The
LOST

ANNE SCHRAFF

SADDLEBACK
EDUCATIONAL PUBLISHING

URBAN UNDERGROUND

SADDLEBACK
EDUCATIONAL PUBLISHING
www.sdlback.com

ISBN-13: 978-1-61651-585-0
ISBN-10: 1-61651-585-6
eBook: 978-1-61247-231-7

Printed in Guangzhou, China
0212/CA21200288

16 15 14 13 12   1 2 3 4 5

CHAPTER ONE

Hey homies, check out that red hot convertible!" Paul Morales pointed as he walked with his friends toward Hortencia's restaurant and tamale shop. All three boys wore hoodies in the cool night. They stopped and watched the car go by. "Whoa!" he yelled. "Check out the chick at the wheel! She's even hotter!"

Carmen Ibarra was driving the convertible. It was a birthday gift from her parents for her seventeenth birthday. It was a used convertible, but it was still nice. Carmen was shocked at how the dark-haired boy was yelling at her. Carmen was a pretty girl. She had big, brown eyes and cascading reddish brown hair to her shoulders. But she didn't consider herself one of the real hotties at Cesar Chavez High School, where she was a junior.

"So many other girls are more striking than I am," she thought. "Girls like Naomi Martinez and even Mira Nuñez. They get a *lot* of attention from the boys." Both of those had handsome boyfriends. But Carmen never had a serious boyfriend. She hung out with boys and danced and went to parties with them. But she never paired off with one special boy.

Carmen's twenty-year-old sister, Lourdes, was in the car too. Lourdes was in college. "Carmen," she asked in a critical voice, "do you *know* those boys?" One of the guys wore a white T-shirt and skinny jeans. The other two wore baggy clothing. They all looked as though they might be gangbangers.

"No, I've never seen them before in my life," Carmen answered. But the tallest boy, who looked kind of cute, seemed vaguely familiar. She thought that he might have been a senior when she was a sophomore. But, if it was him, he looked much different now. He looked taller and tougher.

The convertible stopped in front of Hortencia's. Lourdes and Carmen got out of the car and walked toward the tamale shop. Two of the boys stood on the sidewalk, watching them. The tall one moved away from the other two and came up to Carmen. "Remember me?" he asked.

"Uh no," Carmen replied, "I don't think so." Carmen was well-known for being a chatterbox and talking too much. But right now the boy intimidated her. She wasn't used to guys yelling that she was "hot," especially not a handsome boy like this one. She was embarrassed and thrilled, both at the same time. The hair stood up on the nape of her neck.

"I'm Paul Morales," he explained. "I graduated from Chavez last year. I think you were in the tenth grade. I kept noticing the girl with the big, brown eyes. But hey, you've changed. You're smokin'. I go to the community college now. I'm learning computers and film."

Lourdes Ibarra was attractive but not as pretty as Carmen. She chimed in. "I'm Carmen's sister. I'm studying nursing at State."

"Great," Paul responded. "We need all the pretty nurses we can get. They're what saves a guy when he gets sick and stuck in a hospital. Without cute chicks taking care of us, we'd just forget it and jump out the windows."

Lourdes looked at Carmen nervously. The young man made her uncomfortable.

"Well, nice to have met you," Lourdes ended the conversation. "Carmen and I are going in to have our tamales now."

Inside the shop, the girls ordered their tamales and found a table. Carmen's face felt very warm. She was shaken by the encounter, but it was fun too. She often saw guys at Chavez come on to girls like that. But none had ever happened come up to her. She felt excited now and strangely special.

The three boys came in too, sat at the counter, and ordered. Paul Morales turned around occasionally and glanced at Carmen. He smiled a little. Carmen got goose bumps.

"I don't like them," Lourdes announced in a grim voice. "Those guys creep me out. Did you notice Paul Morales has a tattoo on the back of his hand? A lot of gang members are tattooed. He has a snake tattoo."

Lourdes shuddered. She was seriously dating a young man named Ivan Redondo. He was a college student. He was tall and skinny, and he wore glasses. Carmen thought Ivan Redondo was awful. Oh, he was a nice enough guy. But he was about as exciting as a limp salad. He seemed like a nerd to Carmen. But the girls' father, Emilio Zapata Ibarra was very strict with his daughters. To their father, Lourdes's nerdy boyfriend was ideal.

"I don't think they mean any harm," Carmen objected.

Paul Morales glanced back at Carmen several times. Every time he did, she got bigger goose bumps. She loved Hortencia's tamales. They were the tastiest in the *barrio*. But right now she scarcely knew what she was eating. She kept sneaking glances at Paul. She liked his blue-black longish hair and his big shoulders. Paul took his hoodie off. Under his T-shirt was a marvelously ripped torso. His eyes were kind of disturbing, but not in a bad way. They smoked and flickered like a fire.

Then the other boys removed their hoodies. "Look," Lourdes remarked in a frightened voice. "Their heads are shaven! That's bad. That's a sure sign they belong to a gang. Look, one of them has a tattoo on his head! Ugh!"

"Oh, a lot of boys shave their heads now," Carmen objected. "It doesn't mean they belong to a gang."

"Carmen," Lourdes commanded, "don't look in their direction. You're en-couraging them. That Morales boy keeps giving you sly grins. Don't let him see you smiling. Carmen, *why are you smiling*?" Lourdes had an accusatory look in her eyes. "You're not smiling at him, are you?"

"Oh no," Carmen lied. She kept reliving the first moment she saw Paul. She kept hearing his words. "Check out the chick at the wheel. She's even hotter!"

Carmen liked a lot of boys at Chavez High. A few months ago, she met Ernesto Sandoval. He had been born in the *barrio*, moved to Los Angeles with his parents ten years ago, and recently returned. He really caught Carmen's eye. But Ernesto quickly fell for Naomi Martinez. Now they were a couple, walking around school hand in hand. Carmen liked other boys too, and they became friends. But no boy really, *really* liked her the way she liked some of them.

Carmen wanted a boy to look at her as Ernesto looked at Naomi. She wanted someone to think she was the most beautiful creature on earth. She wanted a boy who thought she was precious beyond measure.

Carmen wanted a boy to put his arms around her, as Abel Ruiz put his arms around Claudia Villa. Carmen didn't want a great big serious relationship. She just wanted a boyfriend who thought she was special.

"Carmen," Lourdes cautioned, "you've got to be careful around here. There are some really unsavory characters hanging around. And they're looking for girls."

"I know," Carmen responded. "I can take care of myself." Carmen didn't know exactly what an "unsavory character" was. But she wouldn't mind a boy a little more exciting than Ivan Redondo.

When they were finishing their tamales, Carmen cautioned her sister. "Lourdes, don't mention to our parents what happened here tonight. You know how Papa gets."

"He ought to know that a gangbanger was hitting on his daughter," Lourdes declared sternly.

"Paul Morales isn't a gangbanger," Carmen snapped. "He's a college student.

8

What could be more respectable than that? I just wish you wouldn't say anything."

"Carmen, you're my little sister," Lourdes explained. "I have to watch out for you. You don't have a big brother to look after you, so . . ."

"Lourdes, that's sweet," Carmen interrupted. "But honest, I don't need looking after. You can ask anybody at school. I'm strong and I'm tough. Nobody gets the best of me."

The two sisters got up. Lourdes got behind Carmen and urged her toward the door faster than Carmen wanted to go. Clearly, Lourdes wanted Carmen away from Paul Morales as quickly as possible.

But Paul was faster. As the girls went out the door, Paul was beside Carmen. "Hey doll," he said to Carmen. "I work at the computer store on Washington. If you need a new iPhone or you wanna see the new gadgets, I'm your guy. Come on in. You'll have my undivided attention."

"Oh, thanks," Carmen replied. She noticed that Paul had a dimple in his chin. She thought it was very cute. Her goose bumps came back. Carmen could sense that the boy really liked her.

Paul Morales stood there, smiling. He called to Carmen as she walked away, "Hey, I voted for your dad." The girls' father, Emilio Zapata Ibarra, had recently been elected a city councilman. "It's great that he made it. He's gonna turn the *barrio* upside down in a good way. And, boy, do we need it. Give him my regards, Carmen."

"I will . . . thank you," Carmen sputtered, getting behind the wheel of the convertible.

"Boy, what a creep," Lourdes commented. "*Let's go!*"

Carmen turned and glared at her sister. Then they pulled away from the curb. After a few moments of driving, she spoke. "He's *not* a creep. Why do you say that, Lourdes? Honestly, he's probably a very nice guy. What's with you, anyway?"

Carmen felt a little annoyed at Lourdes for picking on Paul. "All boys can't be like Ivan," she told her sister. "I mean Ivan is . . . different. He's more like . . . uh, like an older person. He likes opera and symphonies. He can't stand rock or rap. I mean, he watches black-and-white movies for crying out loud!"

"Ivan Redondo is a special and wonderful young man," Lourdes insisted in an aggrieved voice.

"I'm not saying he's not wonderful," Carmen conceded. "But there are very few guys out there like him, you know?" Carmen drove grimly toward their home on Nuthatch Lane.

"Carmen," Lourdes commanded, "you have to be patient. You're only a junior in high school. I know you don't have a steady boyfriend, but that's okay. I didn't have one until I was in college and met Ivan. There's somebody like Ivan out there for you too. But you've got to be patient."

Carmen bit her tongue. She wanted to say, "I don't *want* somebody like Ivan Redondo. If I had to settle for somebody like him, I'd rather be an old maid. I swear to you this. I will never have a date in my life if it has to be with a guy like Ivan. I'd rather go out with a chimp wearing a bow tie."

That's what Carmen wanted to say. But she loved her sister and didn't want to hurt her. So she couldn't say how she really felt about the guy Lourdes loved.

As they pulled into their driveway, Lourdes's face lit up. Ivan's little VW was on the street. He was very considerate. He always parked on the street. That way, the Ibarra family members could use the driveway.

"Oh, Ivan is here!" Lourdes sang out. She was very much in love with Ivan. Like Ivan, Lourdes wore glasses. When they kissed, they often knocked each other's eyeglasses askew. Carmen almost laughed out loud at that a few times. But she'd learned to control herself.

As they neared the door, opera music wafted from the house. Ivan had brought his iPhone over. He had downloaded *La Traviata*. Carmen hated opera because to her it sounded like people screaming at each other. But that wasn't the only reason she disliked it. Operas seemed to go on forever. Regular music ended in a few minutes.

"Hi Ivan," Lourdes called to him.

"Hi Lourdes," he sweetly responded.

They came together and kissed. Lourdes eyeglasses almost flew off, but they caught on her ear. Carmen ran for her bedroom so that they wouldn't see her laughing. On the way, she almost knocked her little sister over in the hallway. Bernadette, nicknamed Bernie, was eleven years old. She was a little Carmen. They saw eye to eye on everything. Bernie trailed Carmen into her room.

"Isn't it gross?" Bernie snarled to Carmen, putting on a sick-looking face. "The geek's been here already for an hour!"

Carmen laughed and gave her little sister a hug. Bernie then scooted off to her own room.

The Ibarras had three daughters and a son. Lourdes was the eldest. Carmen was next, then Bernie, and lastly Mel, who was ten.

Mel's sole mission in life was flying through the air on his skateboard. He was on it for hours on end. You could hear the clatter of Mel and his friends on their skateboards all afternoon and even into the night. They even skated by the light of the moon. Lourdes often commented, "Why does Mel waste his time on that stupid skateboard? Why doesn't he play baseball or basketball or something that leads somewhere?"

Carmen turned up her salsa music and tried to drown out *La Traviata*. She knew she should be studying for the English test tomorrow in Ms. Hunt's class. Ms. Hunt was a very demanding teacher, and Carmen needed to get ready for the test.

But all Carmen could think of was Paul Morales. She thought Paul was the handsomest boy she had seen in ages. The way he seemed a little dark and dangerous made him all the more appealing. As she studied, Paul kept drifting into her mind.

Carmen went to sleep that night thinking about him. She knew she'd probably never see him again. She knew that he probably was just joking in Hortencia's parking lot. He just wanted to get a charge out of a silly little girl in the red convertible. Hitting on her was sport to him. It really didn't mean anything.

If Paul were a student at Chavez High School, things could be different. Carmen would run into him every day, as Ernesto did with Naomi. Something could happen then. A relationship could develop. Still, even if it led nowhere, Carmen thought tonight was exciting and fun. She would remember it.

Half asleep, yet awake, Carmen thought about his suggestion to visit the computer store. Surely he didn't really mean that she'd have his undivided attention. But she did occasionally go to the store to check out the new stuff. It seemed that just about every week some amazing gadget was coming out. You had to keep abreast of the new technology.

Carmen thought she might drop into the computer store this week. She'd check out the latest products. Carmen understood the technology of the iPhone. But she needed to brush up on some of the new apps. Maybe Paul Morales would happen to be working when she came in. If so, it would be fun to let him explain things.

CHAPTER TWO

At breakfast the next morning, Carmen's father was talking about all his plans for his new city council position. He was in high spirits. He seemed delighted by the opportunity to make a difference in the city he loved. Then, as was his practice, Mr. Ibarra turned to his children. He always tried to keep up with what was going on in their lives.

"So, Lourdes," he asked, "did the anatomy test you were worried about come out okay?"

"Yeah, Dad," she responded. "I worried for nothing. I aced it." She was smart. She was not quite as smart as Carmen, but she was more studious. So she often got better grades.

"And Bernie," Mr. Ibarra went on, "are you getting along better with your teacher? I know you're not used to having a man teaching history. But when you get to Chavez, many of the teachers will be men. So you may as well get used to it."

"Mr. Pike is okay," Bernie whined, "But he's such a fuddy-duddy."

Emilio Ibarra laughed. "Fuddy duddies are not all bad," he chuckled. "They're all right sometimes. They keep us on our toes." He turned then to Carmen.

But before she could say anything, Lourdes chimed in. "Papa, you know, last night me and Carmen stopped at Hortencia's for tamales. And there were some creepy boys there really giving us a hard time. They were yelling and making real inappropriate comments and—"

Emilio Ibarra looked immediately alarmed. "What are you talking about, Lourdes? This is very disturbing. Hortencia is very good about keeping bad men from loitering in her parking lot. This is

18

unacceptable. Has Hortencia's become a hangout for bad sorts of people?" he declared, his mustache twitching in concern. He had a very large mustache. When he was upset, it twitched like a feather duster being wiggled with force.

Carmen gave her sister the darkest look she could muster. Then she turned to her father and spoke. "Oh Papa, don't worry. Don't pay any attention to Lourdes. She gets hysterical if she sees a tiny lizard on her bedroom wall. Lourdes loves to make mountains out of molehills. Last night some perfectly nice teenaged boys were just admiring my beautiful red convertible. That's all. Lourdes got all bent out of shape over that. They were college boys . . . nice college boys."

Lourdes snorted, reminding Carmen of a bull pawing the dirt in frustration. "Papa, Carmen is playing it all down. She got all goofy over some ratty-looking boy. This guy, his name is Paul Morales. Well, he looked pretty tough. But his two friends,

19

they had shaved heads and tattoos. And I'm pretty sure they were gangbangers. This Morales character, he yelled that the convertible was hot, but Carmen was hotter. I just don't like boys talking like that to my sister."

Emilio Ibarra's mustache twitched even more furiously. He turned to Carmen. "You're not making friends with gang-bangers are you, *mi hija*?"

"Papa, Lourdes is exaggerating *as usual*," Carmen snarled, snapping her head toward older sister. "This nice college boy gave me a little compliment. And, I don't know, I guess my sister is jealous!"

"Jealous?" Lourdes screeched. "I'm almost engaged to the most wonderful boy in the world. And I'm gonna to be jealous of some sleazy gangbanger on the street?"

"Paul Morales is not a gangbanger," Carmen yelled. She got up from the breakfast table and pushed her chair back hard. The grating sound it made brought her mother, Conchita, racing from the kitchen.

"This is just a totally ridiculous conversation!" Carmen fumed. She gulped down the last of her orange juice and announced, "I'm going to school!"

Carmen stormed back to her room to pick out a sweater to wear. Then something dawned on her. Paul Morales's picture would be in last year's yearbook. She pulled the yearbook from her bookshelf. Flipping quickly through it, she found the big senior photos. There he was. He was so handsome with a big smile, just as he looked at her last night. Under some of the senior pictures, the students' activities and accomplishments were listed, along with their plans and dreams. But under Paul's picture was something short and strange. There were only two words: The Lost. Carmen thought that was strange.

"Carmen?" Her mother, Conchita, peered in the door. "Is everything all right? You seemed pretty steamed at breakfast."

"Everything is fine, Mama," Carmen replied, putting the yearbook back. "It's

21

just that Lourdes overreacts so much. Some nice college guy complimented me last night in Hortencia's parking lot. And Lourdes acts like we were being attacked by aliens."

Conchita Ibarra laughed. "Sisters and brothers! Little sisters, big sisters! It can be a pain. I had nine siblings. We were at war almost constantly, but still we loved each other. My big brother was the worst. He terrorized every boy who ever looked at me. It is a wonder I escaped to marry your father!"

Carmen turned and looked at her mother. Conchita was very beautiful. "Mama, when you first saw Papa, did you know he was the one? Did the earth move beneath your feet?" Carmen asked.

Mom laughed. "Goodness no! Here was this tall boy with shoulder-length hair. And my papa hated him. Even then he had a mustache, though it was not as big as it is now. Everybody in my family thought he was a wild man. But then, little by little, we got to know each other, and we fell in love. Emilio was the most amazing man I ever knew. I still think so."

"I was wondering, Mama," Carmen said. "You and Dad have lived in the *barrio* a long time. Do you know any family named Morales with a son named Paul?"

"I know several families named Morales," Mom replied.

"This guy who kinda liked me last night, the one at Hortencia's," Carmen ventured to say. "His name is Paul Morales. I thought you might know his family."

Conchita Ibarra looked thoughtful. Then she shook her head. "I don't know anybody named Morales who has a son named Paul."

"Oh," Carmen said, turning toward her closet. Mama left the room, still trying to think of a Morales family with a son named Paul. Carmen picked out a blue pullover and put it on. Looking at herself in the mirror, she decided the sweater looked nice. "Maybe," Carmen thought, "after school

I'll go over to the computer store and spend a little time there. Maybe I'll let Paul Morales explain even the apps I know all about."

Carmen usually walked to school. But now that she owned the red convertible, she often drove. On her way to Chavez High, she went over to Bluebird Street, where Naomi lived. Sometimes she gave Naomi a ride, but today she had a secret motive. Naomi seemed to know a lot of the kids at Chavez. Maybe she knew something about Paul.

Naomi was coming down her walk when Carmen pulled up and yelled out the window, "Want a ride, Naomi?"

"Sure thing," Naomi replied, hurrying to get in. "It's kinda damp and foggy this morning, and my hair is weird."

As Naomi got into the car, Carmen looked at her. She thought Naomi was the most beautiful girl in school. Her violet eyes were magical. And her features were perfect. Her skin was flawless. Plus she had a model's figure. Carmen could see why a handsome guy like Paul Morales might yell at Naomi that she was hot. But he said that to Carmen.

"Naomi," Carmen began, "last night my sister and I went to Hortencia's. And something really strange happened. This guy was standing there with his two friends. Lourdes thought they were gangbangers, of course. She thinks every guy who isn't as nerdy as her boyfriend is in a gang. But they were just guys. Anyway, this really cute guy yelled that my car was hot but I was hotter."

"Cool," Naomi laughed. "You *are* very pretty, Carmen. You're getting beautiful like your mom."

"Thanks Naomi," Carmen responded. "I'm just ordinary looking. But this guy, his name is Paul Morales. He graduated from Chavez last year. I don't remember him. I was wondering if you might remember him. He's tall, like Ernesto . . . thick, dark hair."

"A dimple in his chin?" Naomi asked.

"You remember him!" Carmen cried.

"Yeah, he's really, *really* good looking," Naomi giggled. "My dad used to get on my case all the time because I was noticing cute guys. He said I was boy crazy, and you know where that led. I remember I was in this special English class. There were sophomores, juniors, and seniors all together. Mr. Waverly taught it. Remember him? A skinny little guy with a high-pitched voice and carrot-colored hair? Well, Paul was in that class. I couldn't help noticing him. I was with Clay Aguirre then. Clay used to get so mad at me for looking at Paul. Once he wouldn't speak to me for three days. I remember we spent a lot of time on *The Catcher in the Rye*."

"I've read that," Carmen noted.

"I guess everybody has," Naomi replied. "But Paul Morales really got into it. He identified with the kid in the book— Holden Caulfield. You remember what a loser this kid was? Alienated and mad at the world, sarcastic. Paul loved it. He said he found his soul mate in Holden. Paul didn't study much. He seemed to be an average student. But he got so fired up in this class. He got the best grade in the room. I think Paul was sorta interested in films. He talked about making a movie about Holden Caulfield or something."

"Naomi," Carmen asked, "do you know anything about his family?"

"No," Naomi answered. "We ran into each other a few times at the vending machines. We said a few words. He never talked about personal stuff. I told him once about my mom wanting to be a nurse when she was young. I asked him if his mom worked. He said he was living on his own. I thought that was weird for a seventeen-year-old, but I didn't say anything."

"When Paul shouted out to me last night at Hortencia's, my sister Lourdes went crazy," Carmen said, shaking her head. "She thinks all boys should be like her boyfriend Ivan."

"He's the guy who likes opera, huh?" Naomi asked. "Dork?"

"Yeah," Carmen responded. "This guy actually wears a shirt and tie when he goes to class. He's twenty years old, but he acts like he's thirty or something. When Lourdes sees normal guys that age she freaks. She acts like we're being attacked or something."

Naomi laughed. "I remember Paul always hung out with street kids. They weren't in gangs, I don't think. But they were just, you know, kinda hardcore. They were a little rougher than . . ." Naomi stopped and looked at Carmen. "Are you sort of into this guy, Carmen?"

Carmen felt her face turn warm. "No," she answered too quickly. "I mean, I hardly know him. I'm just curious, like he's the first guy who ever called me hot. I guess it made my head spin a little. But I don't like him. I mean I don't dislike him either. I'll probably never see him again." Carmen was glad they were pulling into the Chavez parking lot. She didn't know what else to say about the strange feelings swirling inside her.

As Carmen walked into Ms. Hunt's English class, she spotted Ernesto Sandoval. Ernesto had been attending Chavez for just a short time. So he wouldn't have known Paul Morales when he was a senior. But maybe Ernesto knew him from the street. Luis Sandoval, Ernesto's father, often walked around the *barrio*. Mr. Sandoval would start up conversations with guys on the street. He hoped to draw them back into school if they were dropouts. Maybe they—Ernesto and his dad—had run into Paul and his friends.

"Ernie," Carmen asked, "do you know a guy named Paul Morales?"

"I don't think so," Ernesto replied.

"Oh, I just thought maybe you'd run into him," Carmen said.

"Wait a minute!" Ernesto exclaimed. "I think that's the guy who worked with Abel at Elena's Donut Shop."

"Really?" Carmen responded. Abel was a sweet, quiet guy who was Ernesto's best friend. Abel was dating a girl from a nearby private school, Claudia Villa. Carmen vaguely remembered Ernesto and Abel talking about some trouble at that donut shop. It seemed somebody was stealing money. The owner was blaming Abel and the other employees.

"Yeah," Ernesto affirmed. "Check it out with Abel. I think he knows the guy pretty well. They went through a big hassle together down at the donut shop."

Carmen scolded herself for thinking about Paul Morales all during the English test. She hoped she stayed focused enough to pull a good grade. Carmen knew she was making much too much of her encounter with him. Paul Morales was just a trash-talking punk who stood around on street corners talking up the girls. That's what she told herself. Probably, before he was done last night, he'd told half a dozen other girls they were hot too. Carmen told herself she just needed to forget about last night—and Paul. She told herself sternly that she was being a fool.

Still, as soon as the test was over, Carmen went in search of Abel Ruiz. She wanted to find out more about Paul Morales. Abel usually ate lunch with Ernesto and the other boys from the track team. But Carmen wasn't about to ask Abel about Paul Morales in front of everybody. On his way to lunch, Abel stopped at the vending machine. So she waited for him there.

"Hi Abel!" Carmen greeted him in a cheerful, matter-of-fact voice. She didn't want to seem anxious.

"Hey Carmen, how's your dad?" Abel inquired. "I bet he's real busy with his new council job."

"Oh yeah, he's really into it," Carmen responded. Then she asked the question she wanted to ask. "Uh Abel, do you know a guy named Paul Morales?"

"Yeah, sure," Abel answered. "Why?"

31

"Oh, I just met him at Hortencia's last night. He said he graduated from Chavez last year, but I don't remember him. He seemed nice. He said he was glad my dad got elected and stuff. So, you know him, huh?" Carmen asked, fishing for information. Abel had to see that. "He's a pretty nice guy? He seemed to be. . ."

"I like him," Abel told her. "He broke me in at Elena's Donut Shop. He's smart. He's got some temper, though. Our boss, Elena, she kept missing money. Pretty soon she was accusing me and Paul. One time she made us give her our wallets so she could look for her money in there. Then she wanted our pockets turned inside out. Paul really lost it. He yelled at her. Called her names. He quit on the spot."

Abel grinned at the memory and plunked change into the vending machine. "He threatened to throw all Elena's donuts on the floor. He stormed outta there like a tornado. I like the guy, though. You just don't cross him." Abel punched the buttons for a nutrition bar, and the machine delivered his snack.

Carmen nodded. "Ernesto told me about that. They found out the lady's daughter was stealing the money. Well, I can understand Paul getting mad. I'd sure hate to be accused of something I didn't do."

"Yeah," Abel agreed. "I went back to work there. I'm still there—me and Claudia. Elena's brother runs the place now. He's a lazy guy, but he doesn't bother us. Elena's down at Rosarito Beach trying to get her kid to move back here. Sarah's with her dad down there." Abel fished out the nutrition bar from the machine. Then he looked closely at Carmen. "You got something going with this guy, Carmen?"

"Oh no, I was just curious," Carmen protested.

"Carmen," Abel smirked at her, "you got a light in your eyes. That tells me it's not just curiosity. Paul is real good-looking. Chicks notice him. I could see them staring at him in the donut shop. Carmen, I can always tell if a girl has the hots for some guy. She gets *that look*, and you got it."

When school ended that day at Chavez, Carmen knew the sensible thing for her to do. She should drive home and do some homework. Instead, she decided to drive down to the computer store. Maybe Paul would be working there. Maybe he'd turn out as nice as he was last night.

While driving to the store, Carmen didn't know what to expect. If Paul acted as though he'd never seen her before, Carmen would just pretend to be looking at an iPhone. Then she'd split out of there.

Carmen parked in the computer store lot, clinging to his words of last night. She had practically memorized them.

"Hey doll," he'd said, "I work at the computer store on Washington. If you need a new iPhone or you wanna see the new gadgets, I'm your guy. Come on in. You'll have my undivided attention."

Carmen entered the store nervously, looking around.

"Hey Carmen!" Paul called out, popping out from behind a camera display.

"Oh . . . hi," Carmen sputtered. "I was just coming home from school. I wanted to see that new Apple thing. Everybody said it's the best. I don't usually jump on a new trend, but . . ."

Paul Morales wore a bright blue shirt with the name "Washington Electronics" on the back. He looked good in blue. Carmen thought he'd look good in any color. "Well," he said, "step right up and let me show you what it does."

"Oh," Carmen noted, "it's nice and shiny anyway."

"It downloads music, and you can use it to read a book," Paul explained.

"Is it a camera too?" Carmen asked.

"No, it doesn't take pictures," Paul replied.

"It's not a phone either, is it?" Carmen asked.

"No, but let me show you some apps," Paul explained. Carmen let Paul try to sell the Apple gadget. Then she said, "Well, I don't really need something like this. But everybody was talking about it. I just wanted to see what I might be missing. The new stuff is coming out so fast. What you thought was cutting edge last year is already old."

"Yeah," Paul agreed. "Pretty soon they'll be dissolving us into particles and sending us around. Like in the old *Star Trek* show. Remember, 'Beam me up, Scotty'?"

"Yeah," Carmen said.

Paul was looking right at Carmen. He was looking at her so intently that she was getting uncomfortable. Carmen wondered what he might be thinking. . . . "Hey, she was a lot better looking at the wheel of that hot little convertible. Wow, this chick looks better at night than when all the lights are on."

Carmen wanted to flee the store. But then he smiled and said, "Hey, you really *are* cute, doll. I thought about you last night after I went home. Sometimes I'll take a look at a good-looking chick, but I don't dwell on it. But you stuck in my head."

Carmen felt as though she was already dissolving into particles. She thought about him all last night. She couldn't believe that he thought about her too. She thought he was the cutest, most interesting guy she had met in a long time—maybe *ever*.

"So, Carmen," he asked with almost frightening insight, "what makes me think you didn't come in here just to look at this new gadget?"

"What?" Carmen stammered.

"I don't know," Paul said. "Maybe it's just my imagination. But I got the feeling that last night we clicked. We had the karma going for us. Did you get that feeling, Carmen? It's like those moments they have in the old romantic movies. You know, the ones with the actors who're all dead now. The guy looks across the room, and there *she* is. She sees him, and something happens. Am I right, doll?"

"Uh, well," Carmen murmured, "you kinda surprised me last night. You know, when you yelled that stuff. That never happened to me before. It took me by surprise." Carmen laughed a little. "You really had my sister going. She was scared. You and your friends. I mean, boy, she wanted to get out of there fast."

"But you weren't offended, were you, doll?" Paul asked.

"Oh no, no. I thought it was kind of cute." Carmen smiled at him.

"So, Carmen," Paul started to say, "would it be okay if I called you sometime? You don't have a steady boyfriend do you?"

"No, I don't," Carmen answered. Then, to save her pride, she added, "Not right now."

"I could call you then?" Paul confirmed. "No big deal? Just maybe a movie, something to eat. I don't have a hot red convertible. If you wouldn't mind riding in a small pickup, it'd be real cozy for the two of us."

Carmen was scared. It was happening too fast. But she was tempted too. She wanted to give him her phone number.

Carmen pulled out a little paper and scribbled her cell phone number on it. She handed it to Paul.

"Cool!" he nodded.

CHAPTER THREE

At the dinner table that night, Emilio Ibarra was talking about the staff he had just hired. He told everyone how it all was falling into place down at the city council.

"First thing I'm getting underway is that veterans outreach for the weekend," he declared. "We've got to make services available for the guys and gals who served. I got the mayor on my side, and some local doctors and dentists. We're gonna provide physicals, eye exams, dental checkups. If the vets are young and healthy enough, we'll get them job opportunities."

Mr. Ibarra hefted the fork full of food in front of him. "We're gonna get the guys living in the ravine a way to have a permanent address so they get their Social Security. Some of them haven't even been getting the checks coming to them. The government isn't sending the check to a tarp in the ravine. And they can't do direct deposit like most of the seniors do 'cause they got no bank accounts."

Carmen's mother, Conchita, had made delicious chicken *enchiladas*. Carmen usually loved them. But right now she was eating without even thinking how good they were. She had given her phone number to a boy she hardly knew. He was a stranger, a tough young man with a snake tattooed on the back of his hand. Abel said Paul was eighteen, just a year older than Carmen. So his age was okay. But Paul seemed much older because he was so street-smart.

Lourdes was missing from the dinner table. Ivan Redondo had taken her to a symphony. Carmen could not imagine herself going to a symphony. But she was grateful that Lourdes wasn't here. When

41

Carmen mentioned Paul Morales, Lourdes would throw cold water on the whole thing.

When Papa had his say about his new job, he asked each of his children about their days. Carmen finally found the courage to speak up.

"You guys," she said when her turn came, "there's a guy who works down at the computer store. He graduated from Chavez last year. He remembers me as a sophomore, but I don't remember him. Anyway he's in college now, sorta studying filmmaking. He uh . . . asked me if he could call me for a date sometime. He said maybe we could, you know, go to the movies or something."

There was dead silence at the table. Emilio Ibarra's mustache twitched. Finally the man spoke in a grave voice. "Is this the same young man who shouted at you at Hortencia's? The one Lourdes was so concerned about? Is this Paul Morales?"

"Yeah, Dad," Carmen admitted. "I went over to the computer store where he works.

He showed me all the new stuff. He really knows his way around the new technology."

"He's the boy who yelled that you were a hot tamale?" Mr. Ibarra asked. His mustache was twitching even more.

"He didn't say I was a hot tamale," Carmen said in as calm a voice as she could muster. "He just said I was . . . uh, hot."

"I don't like my little girl referred to as hot," Mr. Ibarra declared.

"It doesn't mean anything," Carmen objected. "It's just the way guys talk now."

"I never heard Ivan Redondo refer to your sister, Lourdes, as hot," Emilio Ibarra countered.

Carmen felt like saying, "Ivan Redondo is an idiot." Instead, she told Papa, "Paul is really very nice."

Carmen's father had abandoned eating and now focused entirely on her. "I never heard Ernesto Sandoval call Naomi Martinez hot," he intoned.

"Paul didn't mean anything," Carmen said.

"Lourdes thinks he and his friends are involved with gangs," Mr. Ibarra responded.

"Paul isn't into gangs," Carmen insisted. "He was a good student at Chavez. He was in a special advanced English class. He got the best grade in the room. Now he almost runs that computer store. And he's in college, taking filmmaking classes and all that."

Carmen was getting a headache. Her father was always very strict. When Lourdes was seventeen she wanted to date a boy Papa didn't approve of. Carmen thought that boy was way better than the one she ended up with—Ivan Redondo. But Dad squashed her friendship with a cute, normal guy who liked rock music. Carmen didn't think anything of it at the time. She was fourteen. And she wasn't interested in her older sister's love life. Carmen even thought it was cute and funny how Papa's mustache twitched. That happened whenever he was scolding Lourdes about her rock and roll boyfriend. To Papa, he was just an unworthy boy who was trying to get his precious Lourdes.

But now the shoe was on the other foot. Carmen didn't see anything cute or funny about Papa sitting there scowling at her. She wasn't amused by his twitching mustache. Papa's intent was to drive the cutest, most exciting boy Carmen ever met out of her life.

"What kind of parents does this boy have?" Mr. Ibarra asked. His gravity was that of a man checking the credentials of someone about to be in charge of Homeland Security. He turned to Conchita Ibarra, "*Mi querida*, do you know a Morales family with a son named Paul?"

Carmen's mother shook her head. "No, I don't think so." She'd already been asked that question.

"So then, where do his parents live?" Mr. Ibarra asked.

"Paul is sort of on his own," Carmen answered. She knew such an admission was killing her chances of dating him. She quickly added, "I think his parents are dead."

"Carmen, this eighteen-year-old boy lives on his own? And you *think* his parents are dead? You must know these things before you get involved with him," Emilio Ibarra scolded.

"Papa," Carmen protested in an emotional voice, "I just met Paul. It's no big deal. He's not even my boyfriend. He'll probably never even call me. I've *never* had a boyfriend. Now this nice guy who used to go to my school sort of likes me. And he just wants to take me to some dumb movie. You're acting like some monster from a *Friday the 13th* movie is dating me!"

Carmen's little brother, Mel, piped up. "I ate everything, even the disgusting broccoli. Can I go out now? Jack is coming over, and we're gonna skateboard."

"Do not call the delicious healthful broccoli your mother made disgusting," Mr. Ibarra ordered his son. Papa was already in a cross mood over Paul Morales.

"Why can't we all just chill out?" little sister Bernie suggested, rolling her eyes. "Man, no wonder there's wars!"

Emilio Ibarra glared at all his children. "You do not tell your father to chill out, Bernie. I'm exercising my very important paternal guidance."

"Whatever!" Bernie responded, finishing the *enchilada*. "All I know is, me and Estebán Negrete used to go to Elena's for donuts. Paul would always just get us the fresh ones. He'd see we didn't get no stale jelly donuts. Elena liked to sell the stale ones to dumb kids."

Carmen felt like hugging her little sister. Instead she tried to be reasonable. "Papa, I know you worry about me, but, look, can't you trust me? I've never done anything dangerous or really stupid. I'm a very responsible person. I have strong values, Papa . . ."

47

"You could invite this Paul Morales to the house for dinner, Carmen," Mr. Ibarra said. "Then your parents can get to know him before he takes you out. We will know to whom we are entrusting our precious *hija*."

"You'd scare him away, Papa," Carmen wailed. "Papa, don't you realize how you scare people? Even Ernesto Sandoval was afraid of you when he first met you."

"I scare people?" Mr. Ibarra objected in indignation. "Who am I—Freddy Krueger? Am I some terrible ax murderer? I have just been elected to the city council with a huge plurality of votes. I did not scare all those voters, *mi hija*! But I would scare this boy Morales? He who hangs with boys with shaved heads and has a snake tattooed on his hand?"

"Papa," Carmen cried, "I am seventeen years old. I've never had a real boyfriend in my life. Paul probably won't even call me, and all this is over nothing. But if he does call me, I want to go out with him, Papa!"

Carmen's voice trembled. "He's nice, Papa. He's a good friend of Abel's. Abel wouldn't have a creep for a friend."

Emilio Ibarra leaned back in his chair, looking anguished. He sighed deeply, causing his big black mustache to quiver. He turned to his wife. "*Mi querida*," he asked, "what do you say? She is your child too. You love her as much as I do. I don't want to be unreasonable, but I want *mi hija* to be safe. What do you say?"

"If the boy calls, then Carmen has the right to decide if she will go with him, Emilio," Conchita Ibarra replied. "*Mi esposo*, we raise our children with values and wisdom. But we cannot live their lives for them. We must trust them. I trust Carmen. She has never given us reason not to."

"Thank you Mama, Papa," Carmen said. "And don't worry, Paul will probably never call me. But someday a boy I like will call me, and I want you to trust me."

Carmen went to her room and tried pulling her long, thick hair into a ponytail.

49

She then let it hang loose. She thought her hair was prettier when it hung loose. Last week she had gone to the mall with Naomi, Tessie Zamora, and Yvette Ozono. They all convinced her that her lipstick was too purplish. She needed a softer pink tone. So Carmen bought a new lipstick and tried it. She smiled at the difference it made. Her friends were right. The pink lipstick was nicer against her light brown skin. She added lip gloss, and she felt even prettier.

It was eight o'clock Wednesday night. Carmen was studying for her math class. She had just gone online to look at the problems her teacher had posted. Then her cell phone rang. For just a moment she stared at her phone. Surely it couldn't be Paul Morales.

"Hello?" Carmen said.

"Hi Carmen. Paul." He had a nice, deep baritone voice that went with his wonderful muscular physique. His face leaped into Carmen's mind—the thick blue-black hair, the smoky eyes, the dimple in his chin. The goose bumps popped out all over her.

"Hi Paul," Carmen managed to say.

"You busy this Friday night?" he asked.

Carmen thought to herself, "What's my schedule for Friday night? Watching that old movie on TV? Downloading Beyoncé or the Black Eyed Peas? Fooling around on the computer? Texting her friends about her unexciting life? . . . 'Just fed cat. Yes, she likes new kitty mix.' . . . 'Watching *Titanic* again. Can U believe it?'"

"No, I'm not busy," Carmen answered in less than a second.

"How about if we go to a movie and then stop at some little cool dive?" Paul suggested.

"Okay, that sounds nice, Paul," Carmen agreed. Was she being too eager? Would she be wiser to refuse the first date to whet his appetite? But that wasn't Carmen. She was never into games. She couldn't bother with anything like that. The truth was that she really, *really* wanted to go out with Paul.

51

"Okay," Paul replied. "I'll pick you up around seven. Where do I pick you up?"

"Three twenty-three Nuthatch," Carmen told him. Her heart was pounding. The goose bumps wouldn't go away. "I'm really looking forward to it, Paul."

"Yeah, me too, doll," he said.

Carmen threw her arms around herself and twirled around the room. She went to a lot of parties and danced and had fun. She was a very happy person. She wasn't overeager to have a special boyfriend. Carmen Ibarra was a fun-loving teenager. She had no sense of desperation because she didn't have a boyfriend. She always just enjoyed herself, sure that a great guy would appear eventually. Now she was seventeen. And something had changed. A special guy was in her life, out of the blue. When Paul Morales appeared, she suddenly felt he was special.

Carmen glimpsed her dancing body in the mirror. Her mother was a wonderful dancer, and Carmen was pretty good too.

Carmen was smiling as she spun past her mirror, her reddish brown hair flying.

At breakfast the next morning, Carmen told her parents about Paul. She told them he had called, and they were going to the movies Friday night.

Emilio Zapata Ibarra did not look happy. He had been consoling himself with the hope that the unpleasant boy would just fade away. Maybe, he thought, the boy would never actually call. Conchita reached over and patted her husband on his hand. "It will be fine," she assured him. Carmen was grateful to her mother.

"He will, of course, come to the house and meet us," Carmen's father insisted.

"Oh yes," Carmen said. To herself she said, "Oh please, Papa, don't wear one of those plastic sheriff's badges from the cereal boxes. Please, Papa, don't lecture Paul about what a precious little angel I am. Please don't demand that he bring me home at a decent hour. Please don't ask Paul where his parents are. Please don't ask him about the tattoo of the snake on the back of his hand. Please, please, don't ask him about the snake."

At school on Thursday, Carmen had lunch with her group of friends, Naomi, Tessie, and Yvette.

"I'm going out with Paul Morales Friday night," Carmen announced.

"Oh wow," Naomi remarked, "he's a fast worker."

"We're going to the movies, and then we'll stop for something to eat," Carmen went on. "Dad doesn't know Paul. So he's kind of nervous about it. But Mama convinced him to cool down."

"*Nobody* knows Paul," Tessie commented. "He's kind of a mystery man."

Carmen looked at Tessie. "Why do you say that?" she asked.

Tessie smiled. "Well, I was at Abel's house. He was cooking one of his new dinners. You know he wants to be a chef someday, and he's trying out all the new recipes. Well, Abel's girlfriend, Claudia, was there. She worked with Paul and Abel at Elena's Donut Shop."

Naomi took a sip of her drink. "Claudia told me she really likes Paul, but don't press him about his past. He's real touchy about that. Claudia says he lives in a tiny studio apartment over on Cardinal Street. He's lived there alone for quite a while, and nobody knows him around there. Claudia says it's like he dropped from the skies in a UFO."

"But he did graduate from Chavez last year," Carmen pointed out. "He's in the yearbook and everything."

"That's right, he did," Tessie affirmed. "I had a class with him, the one that Waverly taught. Remember that, Naomi? Remember that amazing report Paul gave. He had the whole class in the palm of his hand. He sort of became the teenager in that J. D. Salinger book. He morphed into Holden Caulfield. Remember him saying adults are all phonies and creeps?"

"Yeah," Naomi nodded. "He loved that book all right."

"What movie are you guys going to see?" Yvette asked.

"I'm going to let Paul pick the movie," Carmen answered. "I like most movies. There's a romantic comedy out that's supposed to be good. But I don't want to drag Paul to some chick flick."

"He'll probably want to see a horror movie," Yvette said. "Most guys want to see horror movies or science fiction with crazy special effects. I had a boyfriend once." A terribly sad look came over Yvette's face. "All he wanted to see were slasher movies. There was nothing too gross and bloody for him."

Naomi and Tessie knew the boy Yvette was talking about. She'd dated a gang member nicknamed Coyote, and he abused her. Then she finally met a nice guy— Tommy Alvarado—and she dropped Coyote for Tommy. Coyote came to Yvette's birthday party and shot Tommy to death before her eyes. For a long time Yvette was so traumatized that she wouldn't even go to school. But Ernesto's father went to her house and gently convinced her to return to Chavez. Now she was making great grades, especially in math.

At that moment, Clay Aguirre came walking by. He used to be Naomi Martinez's boyfriend before he got so angry one night that he hit her. He still hoped he might win Naomi back from Ernesto. Now he smiled at Naomi and commented, "You're looking beautiful as usual, Naomi."

"Thanks," Naomi replied in a flat voice. She didn't want compliments from Clay. She didn't want anything from Clay except for him to leave her alone.

"Hey Carmen," Clay remarked, "now that your old man is in the city council, you guys'll be living large, right?" Clay had worked hard for Emilio Ibarra's opponent.

"No, Clay," Carmen answered. "My father doesn't intend to profit from his job like Monte Esposito did. When my dad ran for city council, he meant to serve the people, not be served by them. That's why the grand jury is investigating Esposito right now. He helped himself, not the people."

"Well, we'll see," Clay laughed. "Want to bet that your old man will be at the trough same as Esposito?"

"Go soak your head, Clay," Carmen snapped. Tessie and Yvette laughed. Clay Aguirre glowered at them as they laughed—at him. He had a look of pure rage on his face as he walked away.

CHAPTER FOUR

On Friday, in the late afternoon, Carmen selected the latest top she had bought at the mall. It was more expensive than most tops she bought. But she'd gotten birthday money from her grandmother, and she felt free to spend a little more. It was a pale blue graphic top with a scoop neck. It looked perfect with the turquoise necklace she had gotten from Ernesto and Naomi for her birthday. Carmen smiled at herself in the mirror.

As seven o'clock approached, Carmen noticed her father pacing around the house like a caged lion. He acted as though something momentous, and possibly ominous, was about to happen. He had not seemed nearly this nervous on election night awaiting the returns for the city council race. A young man he didn't know—a young man his eldest daughter had serious misgivings about—was taking Carmen out.

Carmen felt sorry for her father. She knew he loved her very much, and she treasured his love. Carmen was sure that, whatever happened in her life, she would always have the love and support of her family. That meant the world to her. That was a wonderful feeling. Many kids didn't have such love. Carmen was sorry her father was going through so much anxiety. On the other hand, Carmen believed it was all unnecessary. Her heart told her Paul Morales was a good person.

As the hour approached, Carmen herself was feeling some anxiety. Carmen remembered that Paul had exploded in fury at the donut shop when he was falsely accused of theft. What would happen when Paul Morales saw the big man with the mustache? What would he do when he realized how reluctant Papa was to entrust his precious daughter to Paul? Would Paul just turn around, get back into his pickup, and drive off in a huff?

The pickup pulled into the driveway. Carmen froze. She had seen many boys from school pull into a girl's driveway. They would just hit the horn and wait for the girl to come running out. When Clay Aguirre used to date Naomi, that's what he did. He parked in front of the Martinez house and hit the horn. Sometimes he honked again and again if Naomi was tardy. Naomi loved Clay so much in those days that she put up with that kind of treatment.

But Paul got out of the cab and came walking to the door. He was wearing jeans and a dark green pullover sweater. He looked nice. He not only looked handsome, but he looked nice and conservative.

Conchita Ibarra answered the doorbell. She felt that was best. Emilio Zapata Ibarra was six foot four. His huge mustache was twitching, and his face was red with anxiety. Seeing him was not the best introduction to the family.

"Hello, you must be Paul," Conchita Ibarra said. "Come on in."

"Thanks," Paul Morales said.

"I'm Conchita Ibarra, and this is my husband, Emilio." She made the introductions softly. Emilio Ibarra stepped forward, his face flushed, his mustache in motion. He stared at the young man, thinking he looked pleasant enough. But he looked a little tough. He didn't have that meek look that Ivan Redondo had.

Paul extended his hand. "It's a pleasure to meet you, councilman. I joined the *Zapatistas* early on. Esposito had to go. The people did a smart thing electing you."

Mr. Ibarra took the young man's hand. He gave it a firm shake. "Thank you very much," he responded. He looked at the snake tattoo. He didn't like it.

Emilio Ibarra wanted to say many things. He wanted to ask the young man about his background, his values, his family. But Conchita had warned him about all that. Emilio was a strong man. But he was wise enough to know he would do well to follow his wife's lead. She had a better grasp of parenting than he did. She was protective but not smothering. So he said nothing.

"Paul is here!" Mrs. Ibarra called out. Carmen had been waiting in the hall, terrified of what her father would say. Now she came into the living room.

"Hi Carmen," Paul said. "You look terrific." He turned to Mr. Ibarra. "We'll be home about eleven. I'm a very careful driver. So you needn't worry. I've never had a ticket, and I've been driving since I was fifteen."

"That's good," Mr. Ibarra murmured in a muffled voice.

He then watched his daughter go out the door with a stranger. His heart was pounding. This was not a good night for Emilio Zapata Ibarra. He had done his best not to embarrass his child. He restrained all his natural fatherly concerns. Now he stood at the window as the pickup backed out of the driveway on Nuthatch Lane.

Usually the Ibarras went to bed around ten. They were very early risers. So ten was usually a good time to go to bed. But tonight Mr. Ibarra would not go to bed at ten. He would not go to bed one minute before his child was home.

"So," Paul Morales said as he drove, "you got any movie in mind you'd like to see, Carmen?"

"You pick something," Carmen suggested.

"Okay," Paul nodded. "Let's skip the multiscreen mall. There's a little theater near downtown that plays older movies. I always wanted to see one of those old movies. It's the one about the old man, the kid, and the dog attaching balloons to their house and floating off. I really love animation. Would that be okay? I wanted to see it when it was first run. But stuff came up and I missed it."

"Oh, I never saw that movie either," Carmen remarked. "I'd like to see it. I like animation too. It's come so far since the old Disney movies."

"Well, in this filmmaking class I got, we learn to do amazing things," Paul told her. "It's a whole new world."

"That sounds like an exciting career," Carmen commented.

"Well, I'm a long way from a career," Paul chuckled. "But in this class we get to do short movies. It used to be such a big deal to make even shorts. But with the new cameras and all, man, anybody can shoot a movie. Like that dude and his girlfriend who shot that spooky movie in an old house. It turned out good enough to make money."

When they stopped at a light, Paul turned and looked at Carmen. "What about you, doll?" he asked. "You figured out yet what you want to do with your life? You got dreams? Maybe you want to follow your father into politics?"

"Who knows?" Carmen responded. "I think I'll be one of those college freshmen who don't know where they're going."

Up ahead, under the street lights, Carmen spotted two young men in baggy clothing. One of them had a hoodie on. The other didn't, and you could see his shaved head. He had a blue tattoo on the top of his head.

Paul slowed the truck and yelled out the window, "Hey Beto! Cruz! What's goin' down?" A green van was parked near where the boys stood.

Carmen was uncomfortable. These were the guys Paul was with at Hortencia's. Maybe they were perfectly okay, but they didn't look it. They had looked ominous in Hortencia's well-lit parking lot. They looked even more ominous now under the pale street light.

"We're crashing a party on Starling," the one called Cruz answered, laughing.

"What party? I didn't hear of any party on Starling," Paul asked. He had brought the truck to a full stop now.

"Ramon Mendez is having a birthday party, and he didn't give us no invite. We're his homies, and he forgot about us," Beto told Paul.

"Okay dudes!" Paul called out. "But don't do anything I wouldn't do. Y'hear what I'm saying?"

Both boys laughed. Beto said, "Ain't much you wouldn't do, man."

Paul Morales drove on. "Those are my homies, Cruz and Beto. They got my back and I got theirs," Paul explained.

"Have you known them a long time?" Carmen asked.

"Yeah, a long time," Paul responded. "I'd be pushing up the grass at Holy Cross if it wasn't for them."

Carmen wondered what he meant by that answer. But she didn't press him. Claudia Villa said he talked about things in his own good time. He didn't appreciate being questioned.

They pulled into the theater parking lot and went in to watch the movie. Carmen thought she'd enjoy it, and she did. It was poignant and funny. The animation was wonderful. Afterward, they stopped at a tiny Mexican restaurant that Carmen never knew existed. It was hidden behind a laundry. They had chicken smothered with *mole poblano*. Carmen thought it was one of the most delicious meals she ever had.

"You know," Paul commented, swallowing a bite of chicken, "that crazy lady, Elena, accused me and Abel of stealing her money. So I got outta there. But then I was hard up for a couple weeks, between jobs. I owed some dude money for a gambling debt. It was tough. But Cruz and Beto came through with beans and rice. Those guys are like family to me. They're more family than I've ever had. They're not just my homies. They're *hermanos*."

Carmen thought that still didn't explain why Paul was so close with Cruz and Beto. There had to be something else. But she could only wait until Paul was ready to tell her.

"Friends are great when they stick with you during the hard times," Carmen remarked. "I got some really nice friends at school. Ernesto and Naomi, Tessie, Abel . . ."

"Yeah, Abel Ruiz is pretty cool," Paul asserted. "I quit Elena's Donut Shop, but he stayed. He called me up a coupla times and asked me if I needed a place to crash. I told him I got a place to sleep, but not much bread. That dude came over with a whole ton of these chicken and noodle deals. Between the beans and rice and that, I survived until I got working again."

"That sounds like Abel," Carmen said. "He has a good heart."

At quarter to eleven, the pickup pulled into the driveway on Nuthatch Lane. Carmen pointed. "Paul, did you see the curtain on the front window just move?" She was giggling.

"Your mom?" Paul asked.

"Dad!" Carmen replied. "He's really protective."

Then she turned toward him and added, "I had a wonderful evening, Paul. Thanks for inviting me. I loved the movie and the little restaurant. More than that, you're lots of fun to be with. I mean, I don't know about you. But I had the best time I've had in a long time. I hoped I'd have fun. But I didn't think you'd be so easy to be with. It's like I've known you for a long time. You're just a really nice guy, Paul and I—"

Paul smiled and touched his fingers to Carmen's lips.

"I'm sorry. I talk too much," Carmen apologized.

"Oh, I don't so much mind you talking, doll," he whispered. "But there's something else we need to use our lips for . . . if I'm lucky."

Carmen had kissed boys before. At the many parties at the Ibarra house, she had kissed cousins and friends from Chavez High. She hugged and kissed Ernesto when he joined the *Zapatistas* to help elect her father. But none of those kisses meant anything. Now Carmen raised her face. Paul Morales leaned forward to kiss her gently but firmly on the lips. Then Carmen kissed him again, for good measure. It was her first *real* kiss with a boy.

"Wow!" Paul said. "We've got to do this more often, doll."

Paul walked with Carmen to the door. She turned the key in the door and smiled up at him. Then she went inside. She glimpsed her father's back as he hurried down the hallway. He was trying to escape after spying on the couple from the window. But Emilio Ibarra wasn't fast enough.

"It's okay, Papa," Carmen called to him. "I'm not upset that you were watching us."

Carmen's father turned and came back into the living room. "Did you have a nice time, *mi hija*?" he asked.

"Yeah, Papa, I did," Carmen responded. "We watched a really good movie and ate at a cute little restaurant. Paul was so wonderful."

"He was a gentleman, right?" Mr. Ibarra asked.

"Oh yeah," Carmen assured her father. "Absolutely."

Mr. Ibarra smiled with relief. "Good," he declared. Then he asked, "Did he explain why he has the snake tattooed on his hand?"

"No Papa, and I didn't ask him," Carmen said.

"Maybe he has a pet snake," Mr. Ibarra mused. "Some boys have pet snakes. I never had one myself when I was a boy. You have to feed them live mice, captive mice. This bothered me. When snakes and other wild animals hunt their prey, I believe the prey should have a chance to escape. I don't like feeding captive mice to snakes. It's not sporting."

"I don't think Paul has a pet snake, Papa," Carmen said, interrupting Papa's train of thought.

Mr. Ibarra shrugged. Then he said goodnight to Carmen and finally went to bed.

Carmen hurried to her room in a happier mood than she had been in for a long time. She was usually in a pretty good mood, but tonight she felt unusually wonderful. The minute Paul pointed toward her in Hortencia's parking lot, she was intrigued. He was so cute and so edgy. He wasn't just a nice looking guy. He was deliciously different, mysterious, and off the wall. The fact that Lourdes was afraid of him was like icing on the cake.

"Carmen?" Lourdes came out of her room in her pajamas and peered into Carmen's room. "How was it?"

"Oh, it was great, Lourdes," Carmen said in a hushed tone. "It was even better than I'd hoped it would be. We had fun, and he was so nice and romantic. I hope he calls me again. I think he will. He seemed to have a good time too."

Lourdes stood there, a perplexed look on her face. "He kind of makes me nervous. I was really surprised that Papa let you go out with him. I mean, alone on the first date.

I thought Papa would want you to be with other people on the first date so that . . ."

"So that they could protect me, right?" Carmen asked in a snippy voice.

"Well, yeah," Lourdes admitted. "I thought maybe he'd connect with those horrible friends of his with the shaven heads. You know, he could be all over you, and what would you do? I was really worried."

"He wasn't all over me, Lourdes," Carmen assured her sister. "We had a nice, sweet kiss, and it was so cool. I mean, I felt like I was standing under a sky full of billions of stars. I heard beautiful music playing. And I was just blown away. It was maybe the best night in my whole entire life."

"Well, he's nothing like Ivan," Lourdes commented.

Carmen thought, "Thank heaven for that! If somebody like Ivan Redondo tried to take me out, I'd run so fast I'd be in the next county before sunrise."

"Ivan Redondo isn't my kind of guy," was all Carmen said.

Lourdes looked at Carmen with narrowing eyes. "I guess I really don't know you, Carmen," she responded before turning and going back to bed in her room.

Carmen pulled down the Chavez High School yearbook from when she was a freshman and Paul was a junior. She was anxious to see what he looked like then. She thought she might even find more pictures of him, playing sports or something. But she was disappointed to find no mention of him in that yearbook. That meant he must have come to Chavez as a senior. He must be from somewhere else, Carmen thought. That's why nobody in the *barrio* knew much about him.

Carmen wondered if his parents were really dead. Or did he leave home and become emancipated? Some young people do that because of a bad situation at home.

Carmen had sweet dreams when she went to bed. She fell asleep thinking about

Paul Morales. She thought about how he laughed at the funny parts in the movie. She recalled how he frequently smiled at her when they talked. He seemed to be really interested in what she had to say. He didn't seem annoyed even when Carmen talked too much, as she often did, even when she went on and on.

That night, she dreamt of Paul.

CHAPTER FIVE

At school on Monday, Carmen parked her red convertible. As she got out of the car, she thought to herself how wonderful it would be if Paul were a student here. She could talk to him during the day. They could eat lunch together, as Ernesto and Naomi often did.

As Carmen was walking to her first class, Clay Aguirre caught up and began walking beside her. "Hey Carmen, I thought your old man was so strict. But looks like he don't mind if his daughter hangs out with low-life trash. Mira seen you riding in Paul Morales's truck Friday night. And she says you guys were all hot and heavy."

Carmen felt the rage rising in her body and turning her face warm. She knew that Clay hated her. Carmen was one of Naomi's friends who urged her to dump Clay when he punched her in the face. Naomi needed the support of people who cared about her so that she'd have the courage to end the abusive relationship. "You fool, you *bobo*," Carmen spat at him. "Paul Morales is a good person. He's not some creep like you who doesn't know how to treat girls."

"Morales is a gangbanger," Clay taunted. "He hangs with that crowd. One of these days he'll be shooting up the streets, girl. And you'll be right in the middle of it."

As Clay Aguirre was yelling at Carmen, Ernesto Sandoval and Abel Ruiz came by. Ernesto glared at Clay. "What's goin' down, dude? You harassing Carmen? Don't be doing that, man, 'cause she's our friend."

"Yeah," Abel Ruiz seconded his friend. "Cut it out."

Ernesto had no respect for Clay. He'd mistreated Naomi when they were dating. Now he was being rude to his new girlfriend, Mira Nuñez. Clay was an arrogant troublemaker.

"Carmen's hooked up with Paul Morales," Clay snarled. "He's a gang member. He hangs with Cruz Lopez and those other wannabes with their shaved heads. Carmen's old man tries to be such a straight arrow. Why's he letting her go with scum like Morales?"

"Paul doesn't belong to no gang," Abel asserted. "I worked with him at the donut shop. He's just a regular guy. He goes to college and works hard every day. Clay, waddya want to be spreading lies for? I went to the auto show with Ernie. Then I went with Paul too, and we had a blast."

"He try to rip off the cars?" Clay asked sarcastically.

"No," Abel groaned. "Don't be talking trash, man. That's why a lot of guys don't like you, dude. You spend all your time dissin' people."

"You'll see," Clay assured them, backing off a little. Clay looked right at Carmen and told her, "Yvette Ozono hung with a dude like Morales. And you know what happened to that stupid chick. Her next boyfriend got offed, and now no guy will even look at her. She's poison."

"Aguirre," Carmen snapped, "why don't you just go soak your head in the birdbath? Maybe it'd wash the dirt out of your mouth."

When Clay walked away, Ernesto turned to Carmen. "I didn't know you were dating Paul Morales."

"Yeah," Carmen explained, "we went out for the first time Friday night. It was great. He's really fun to be with, Ernie. He's different from any boy I ever met."

Abel said, "I'm glad I caught you, Carmen. I'm going to my girlfriend's house on Sunday, the Villas. I'm cooking dinner for them. Me and Claudia and her parents.

I'm thinking it'll be kinda awkward. It'd be just me and Claudia and the older people, you know, the parentals. So it'd be nice if there was another couple our age. So maybe you and Paul could come, Carmen. It'll liven things up. Otherwise I'll be there with Claudia's parents trying to make small talk with older people. And I'm not good at that. They'll think their daughter is dating a jerk, you know."

"Oh Abel, that'd be fun," Carmen said. "Boy, you're really serious about this chef stuff, aren't you?"

"I sure am," Abel responded, "and I want it to be really good for Claudia's folks. Say, listen, it's not really dinner, more like a fancy lunch. But we're havin' it early 'cuz Mr. Villa goes to bed early. Maybe like twelve or so?"

Ernesto laughed. Turning to Carmen, he affirmed, "You're in for a treat, Carmen. Abel had my family over to his house for a salmon dinner. It was the best meal I ever had. Everybody went nuts over it."

"I wonder if Paul would come," Carmen said. "I could call him and—"

Abel grinned and held up his hand to stop her from talking. "No need to, Carmen. I already invited Paul. He said he'd come if you were there. He said he'd like to see Claudia again too, 'cause we all worked together, you know, at the donut place. But Paul said he's not too anxious to be with parents and stuff. He said I'll be looking into Claudia's eyes. So he wants his chick there too so he can look into her eyes."

"Oh," Carmen said, her face turning warm again.

"What're you gonna be cooking man?" Ernesto asked.

"I haven't got the whole menu worked out yet," Abel answered. "But I want it to be awesome. I want to impress Claudia's parents. They want her to get a nice solid boyfriend with good prospects. If they think I'm on my way to being a master chef, I got it made. I want them to like me, 'cause then Claudia and me got an easier time, you know. I'm thinking roasted duck with mushrooms, and maybe butternut squash. My aunt and me tried that. It was pretty great."

Ernesto looked at Carmen. "You lucky girl," he said.

Abel headed off in another direction for his first class, giving Carmen a chance to talk with Ernesto. Ernesto was never Carmen's boyfriend, but she trusted him and liked him. She often talked to him about things that were important to her, and she trusted his judgment.

"Ernie," she began, "Paul and I went to the movies on Friday night. On the way there, he stopped the truck and talked to these two guys in baggy clothes. I've seen them before. They were at Hortencia's that night. He said their names were Cruz and Beto. Paul seemed to be really close to them. He said they helped him out when he lost his job at the donut place. I'd never say this in front of that creep Aguirre. But I've got to admit it, those guys *do* look kinda tough. Do you know anything about them?"

"Uh, I know who you mean, Carmen," Ernesto responded. "I've seen them with Paul too. I think maybe Paul hasn't had the kind of strong family life that you and I and Abel have. I don't know exactly what's going on with him. But I think he's a loner."

Ernesto paused for a moment, thinking. "When you've got no real family you bond tighter with friends, and they become your family. My dad, he's always telling me not to judge people by how they dress. Yeah, gangbangers wear baggy clothes too. And they shave their heads sometimes, but a lot of good guys look that way too. I've never heard of Cruz and Beto getting busted for anything."

"Yeah," Carmen said, smiling at Ernesto. "I know one thing. Paul is awfully nice, and I'm willing to trust him."

"Abel likes the guy, and that's good enough for me," Ernesto added.

When Carmen went to Ms. Hunt's English class, she felt much better. She now could look forward to dinner with Paul and Abel at the Villas. It was always exciting to see what Abel cooked up. And having Paul there too would be a very special experience.

Later that day, Carmen texted Paul. "Abel said U & I are dining Sunday @ Villas."

Paul texted back a happy face.

Carmen giggled and met up with Naomi, Tessie, and Yvette for lunch.

"You're glowing, Carmen," Naomi remarked. "Friday must have been good."

Carmen broke out in a silly grin and nodded her head yes.

As they began eating their lunches, Carmen glanced at Yvette, having a strawberry yogurt. Carmen thought about Clay Aguirre's cruel words. Was Yvette really poison to the guys at Chavez? Did they hold it against her that she'd dated Coyote? Do they think that, by going with Tommy

Alvarado, she'd gotten the boy killed? That was so sad.

Naomi and Tessie left before the lunch period was over. So Carmen and Yvette were alone for a little while before the bell rang. Carmen thought Yvette had to know a lot about the gang scene in the *barrio* from the time she spent with Coyote.

On a spur-of-the-moment impulse, Carmen asked Yvette about Paul's friends. "Did you ever hear of a guy named Cruz Lopez or a guy named Beto? I don't know his last name. They're Paul's friends."

Yvette was silent for a few seconds, and Carmen held her breath. What if either of those boys were friends of Coyote? Carmen didn't know what she would do. Finding out something like that would really disappoint her.

"I know Beto Ortiz," Yvette finally said. "He uh . . . got in a fight with Coyote once."

Carmen turned cold. Beto *was* mixed up with Coyote! Paul's good friend, his homie, was mixed up with a vicious murderer like

Coyote! Carmen began to shiver even though it was a warm day. "Yvette, is Beto . . . in a gang or something?" she asked, terrified of hearing the answer.

"I don't know. I don't think so," Yvette replied. She looked very sad. "We were at the deli, me and Coyote, and this guy came along. I didn't know who he was then. Anyway, Coyote was slapping me around. He did that . . . often. I sometimes . . . shoplifted stuff for Coyote. Sometimes he didn't like what I got . . . you know, like the wrong cigarettes. Then he would hit me. Anyway, this guy—the one I found out was Beto Ortiz—he was just coming along. He yelled at Coyote to stop hitting me."

Yvette had been looking down at her hands. Now she looked up, directly at Carmen. "Coyote . . . he . . . he went at Beto with a switchblade. I almost died. I was so scared. But Beto, he gave Coyote some kinda karate chop and took the switchblade. He got Coyote down on the ground. He twisted his arm behind his back so Coyote was screaming in pain. Beto looked at me and yelled at me to go home, and I did. I ran all the way home. I never saw Coyote scared of anybody before, but he was scared of this guy. Coyote was a dirty coward. He only picked on the weak. That's why he hid in the bushes and killed my Tommy that night. He ambushed Tommy."

Carmen wasn't sure how she felt. She was relieved that Beto Ortiz had not been mixed up with Coyote. But he was still a tough customer.

Yvette added something. "Carmen, I think Coyote mighta broken my nose or hurt me bad that day. So . . . Beto did me a favor."

Sunday at eleven thirty, Paul Morales arrived at the Ibarra house. He was there to pick up Carmen for dinner at the Villas. As he had done before, Paul rang the doorbell and came into the house to wait for Carmen.

Carmen wasn't quite ready. She had been putting on her lip gloss, and it had smudged. So Paul sat in the living room of the Ibarra house. Carmen's little sister, Bernie, looked right at him and told him, "You look like that cute cop on *CSI*."

"Thanks," Paul said, grinning at the girl.

Lourdes was waiting for her boyfriend, Ivan, to pick her up too. They were going for a drive. The tall, thin, bespectacled young man came in and looked at Paul. His expression made it clear that he had heard bad things about Paul from Lourdes. Ivan seemed a little nervous.

Fortunately, Emilio Ibarra had gone to a meeting at church. So it fell to Conchita Ibarra to introduce the two young men. "Ivan, this is Paul Morales, a good friend of Carmen's. Paul, this is Ivan, Lourdes's boyfriend."

"Hello Paul," Ivan said.

"Hey Ivan," Paul replied absently. Paul was looking down at his own hand. He seemed to be admiring the snake tattooed on it.

Mrs. Ibarra then went down the hallway to see how Carmen was doing.

"I attend the university," Ivan stated. "I'm a junior there. I take mostly science classes. I don't know where it'll lead. I think I may become a researcher."

"Great," Paul responded, looking even more intently at the snake on the back of his hand.

"You're in college too, right?" Ivan asked.

"Yeah, community college. It's way cheaper," Paul answered.

"Do you think you're getting a good education there?"

"Oh yeah, sure," Paul asserted, looking toward the hallway. He was trying to will Carmen to appear soon.

Finally Carmen was coming toward them. Just then, Ivan Redondo commented, "Uh Paul, excuse me for asking. But that's an unusual tattoo on the back of your hand. It almost looks like a rattlesnake."

"Yeah, right, that's what it is, a rattler," Paul responded.

"Why did you choose a rattlesnake tattoo?" Ivan asked.

Carmen heard the question, and she felt like smacking Ivan over the head with her purse. How could he be so rude as to pry into Paul's personal choices?

"Oh, I like snakes," Paul said, his voice dripping with sarcasm. "Snakes are cool, don't you think, Evan?"

"Ivan, not Evan," he corrected Paul. "Actually I'm afraid of snakes. I think they're vile."

"Vile?" Paul repeated the word. His eyes were smoking now. Carmen was seeing a side of him she had never seen before. He was getting steamed. Carmen remembered what Abel had said about Paul. He was a nice guy, but you didn't want to cross him.

"Vile?" Paul repeated the word again. "I can't imagine why you'd say such a thing about a member of the snake community.

'Vile' is mean and despicable. Snakes just follow the laws of nature, *Evan*." Paul emphasized the name. "Only human beings can be vile. We perform mean and despicable acts sometimes, but snakes just do what comes naturally."

Paul turned then and looked at Carmen, "You're even more beautiful than I remembered, doll. Come on, let's go."

Ivan Redondo watched Paul Morales go out the door with Carmen. He heard the doors slam shut and the engine started. He was really surprised at Emilio Zapata Ibarra. He was allowing his seventeen-year-old daughter to keep company with such a young man.

As the pickup headed for the Villa house, Carmen asked Paul, "What was that about snakes? I just heard the tail end of the conversation."

"Oh, that dude Redondo," Paul responded, "he seemed upset that I have this snake tattoo on my hand. I guess he has it in for snakes or something. He seemed to think snakes are vile. Evil. That's pretty ridiculous. No animal is capable of evil. Only humans can do stuff like that. I like nature. I like all the animals, even the weird ones."

Carmen wondered why Paul had the snake tattooed on his hand too. But she would never ask him about it outright. As they drove the short distance to Wren Street, she hoped he would offer an explanation. Finally, Paul spoke, as if he'd read Carmen's mind. "It was something that happened out in the Anza-Borrego Desert a while back. You know, the state park? You ever been there, Carmen?"

"Yeah, we go every spring, especially when it's rained a lot. The wildflowers are so beautiful," Carmen answered. "I love it out there. It's so stark and pure."

"Well," Paul went on, "me and Cruz and Beto took a dune buggy out there. When the sand got too deep, we started hiking. We were having a great time when I did a real smart thing. I was poking around under a rock 'cause I saw something move. Anyway, a rattlesnake was sleeping there. He woke up with a start and—ouch, man! He got me, Carmen. He didn't mean to bite me. He was scared, and he was defending himself."

"Oh Paul!" Carmen cried. "A rattlesnake bit you?"

"Yeah," Paul nodded. "I thought, 'Okay, so this is how it all ends. Out here in the Anza-Borrego at the age of seventeen.' Well, Beto stayed with me, said to be still. Cruz ran for the dune buggy. We'd called nine-one-one. But getting me from where I was woulda taken a lot of precious time. Cruz brought the dune buggy fairly close, and the guys carried me to it. We met the paramedics out on the main road, and I got to the emergency room real fast. Luckily, they saved me."

Paul laughed as he watched the road ahead. "So, you see, my homies saved me. I owe my life to them. They took care of me. I wanted to remember what happened that day, so I got the rattler tattooed on my hand. Now, every time I look at it, I remember. I don't want to ever forget *mis hermanos*."

"Wow, what an experience!" Carmen exclaimed.

Paul glanced at Carmen. "You afraid of snakes?"

"No," Carmen answered, "but I respect their territory. When we go hiking in the Anza-Borrego, I've seen rattlesnakes. I just give them lots of room. I know that's their home, and I'm just a visitor. So I don't go snooping around too close."

"Smart girl," Paul nodded. "Poor Ivan, he's really antisnake."

"Well, Ivan is something else," Carmen agreed, giggling. "One time about a month ago, a lizard got in our house when Ivan was visiting. This little guy is scampering across the wall. Ivan and Lourdes are listening to an opera—I think it was *La Bohème* . . ."

"Opera!" Paul gasped dramatically, shuddering in a comic way.

"Yeah," Carmen giggled, "they listen to it all the time. So anyway, Ivan sees this lizard, and he screams louder than the guy's screaming in the opera. He jumps up and runs out the door. He's acting like our house's been invaded by deadly serpents or something. He's outside, looking in the window. He won't come back in until Bernie and me chase the poor little lizard out."

Carmen giggled some more and then spoke. "Oh Paul, I feel like a meanie making fun of Ivan like this, because he really is a nice person."

Paul laughed. "Yeah, he seems okay. Not the kind of a guy you'd want to have a beer with but . . ."

"My sister's really in love with Ivan," Carmen added. "They're so much alike. Me, I'm more like my sister, Bernie. My little brother, Mel, he's just like from another planet. All he wants to do is race around on his skateboard. We're brothers and sisters, but we're all so different." Carmen thought maybe, if she talked about her family, she might get Paul to share something about his own family.

But Paul just smiled and said, "You've got a nice family, Carmen. I think your dad would be just as glad if I signed up for the space program. Maybe I'd take off on a five-year mission to Mars. But, hey, I don't hold that against him. He loves his kids. He worries about them. That's a beautiful thing. If I were your dad, I wouldn't be too crazy about me either. I take some getting used to, doll."

About then, they pulled up to the little house on Wren Street where the Villas lived. The Villas were lower-middle-class people, struggling to advance their daughter to a better life. That was why they sacrificed to send her to a private school. They wanted something better for Claudia than struggling day after day just to stay one jump ahead of the bill collectors.

Carmen spotted Abel's car parked in the driveway. "I see the chef has arrived," Carmen noted, laughing.

"I love that guy," Paul commented. "He's kind of a mousy dude. And how he took all that stuff Elena handed out at the donut shop. He just took it. But lately, he's been coming into his own. He told me this dude, Ernie, encouraged him to go for his dream. That's what friends are for, Carmen. They fill up the holes in your life where your family don't measure up. Friends, *amigos*, one of life's real gifts."

CHAPTER SIX

The Villas greeted Paul and Carmen at the door. Ursula and Matt Villa, Claudia's parents, smiled warmly. Carmen knew quite a bit about them from what Abel had told her. Matt had been a surfer in his youth. He'd been a big, bronzed boy who loved the ocean. He'd dreamed of opening a surfing-related business near the beach. Ursula was a quiet young woman, carefully molded by her own parents not to take risks. When the two married, Matt was expected to get a good, safe job and take care of his family. Now Matt Villa stood there, a bulky, kindly looking man. He was a salesman who hated his job with a passion but who loved his family with even more passion.

Both parents now had just one dream: a good life for Claudia.

"Mom," Claudia said, "these are my friends. I got to know them through Abel. Carmen Ibarra and Paul Morales. Carmen's dad was just elected to the city council. Paul and Carmen are good friends."

"Come on in," Ursula Villa said, smiling at Carmen and Paul.

"Oh!" Claudia sighed. "The aromas coming from the kitchen! You guys! Abel was here so early. He brought this garlic and sprigs of thyme, oyster mushrooms, and butternut squash. He marinated the duckling for the last half hour in the fridge! He's so amazing."

"I'm telling you, Claudia," Paul declared, "this dude is gonna be famous someday. He's gonna end up on television grinding pepper and tossing in spices. Move over, Bobby Flay, or whoever's around then."

They sat in the living room, Paul and Carmen, Claudia and her parents. The

Villas had met Abel before as their daughter's boyfriend. At first they were a little leery of Claudia's dating a boy from Chavez High School. They'd hoped she'd find a boyfriend in the private boys school near her academy. But now they liked Abel very much. They also knew that Carmen Ibarra was the daughter of the new member of the city council.

They felt honored to have the councilman's daughter coming to their humble house for dinner. But they didn't know much about the young man with the snake tattooed on the back of his hand. He was handsome enough, to be sure. But he certainly wasn't the kind of a boy they'd have liked their daughter to be dating.

"So, how does your father like being on the city council so far?" Matt Villa asked Carmen.

"He still sorta can't believe it," Carmen answered. "He's set up his first project already. They had a weekend fair for homeless veterans. They're trying to get medical and dental care and jobs, if they're well enough to work. And they also had a clear-inghouse for cheaper housing. A lot of guys are really hurting, and an outreach like that's a big help. It's easy for the older veterans to just give up and think that nobody cares."

"That's wonderful," Ursula Villa commented. "That's really wonderful. When I'm driving Claudia to school, I sometimes see these sad men. Their signs say that they're veterans, and they'll work for food or something. My father was in the Vietnam War, and he came home with a lot of mental problems. Nobody thought about that, though, at the time. He just struggled along. Then he died . . . he died way before his time. We often wondered if something could have been done for him."

"The old councilman, Monte Esposito, he's a crook," Paul Morales declared. "The grand jury is looking into some of his deals now."

"I never served in any wars," Matt Villa announced. "But I took my turn in the National Guard." He looked at Paul then. "I suppose your dad did the same . . . maybe went to Iraq or Afghanistan?"

"No," Paul replied. That was all he said. A simple no.

Carmen was getting a little nervous. She was glad when Abel appeared to announce that dinner was ready.

They all sat at a pretty walnut table with a nice centerpiece of yellow and orange flowers. The duck was beautifully presented with a golden brown skin. The squash was caramelized, buttered, and seasoned.

Abel served prepared plates directly to the table, and then sat down at his place. The table grew quiet as the diners began to eat. Everything tasted as well as it looked.

During the meal, Carmen noticed that Claudia's gaze rarely left Abel. She could tell that Claudia really liked him. Carmen was so happy for Abel. He had found a lovely, sweet girl who appreciated him. For a very long time, Abel's parents, especially his mother, saw him as the loser in the family. His brother, Tomás, was both better looking and smarter. He had numerous friends, and Abel was a little bit of a loner. Abel felt bad, but he acted the part of the second-rater until recently. Since he embraced his love of cooking, he had become somebody in his own right. Even his bland personality blossomed.

Abel had come into his own.

"Abel," Matt Villa declared, "you are really an excellent cook. It's amazing that a young fellow like you can do this."

"It's wonderful!" Ursula Villa agreed. "Where did you learn to cook like this?"

"I'm studying a lot," Abel explained, his fork poised between his plate and mouth. "I watch the cooking shows on TV, and I read a lot of books. My Aunt Marla helps me too 'cause she lets me try stuff out at her place."

Abel took a mouthful of the delicious meal, chewed, and swallowed. Then he continued. "The only problem I've got is paying any attention to my regular classes at Chavez. I'm so into this cooking stuff that nothing else seems important. But I'm doing my duty at school. I wanna graduate with a fairly decent average. Then I'm going to culinary school. I'm really excited about that."

"Dude," Paul Morales announced, "the way you cook already, you should be a teacher at that culinary school."

Abel took it all in, smiling broadly. He was not a handsome boy. His face was too thin, and just recently he'd begun to heal from a chronic acne problem. His new-found happiness in cooking seemed to assist even with his skin health. Best of all, he had Claudia Villa. Abel cared deeply for her. All during the meal, they exchanged sweet, intimate looks.

Later, Carmen and Paul, at the door, thanked the Villas for having them. They also thanked Abel for the wonderful meal.

"I should thank you guys for coming," Abel objected. "You're my guinea pigs. I'm practicing on you so I'll be ready for the big time."

"Anytime, bro," Paul said. "I'll be a guinea pig whenever the food is this good. If this is what it feels like to be a guinea pig, I volunteer!"

Then Paul asked Abel, "How are things going down at the old donut shop?"

Abel laughed. "That big heavyset guy is still coming in and ordering three dozen donuts. He still takes forever to pick them all out. He's still holding up the line. But Claudia is great in helping out with the disgruntled customers. She keeps everybody happy while I try to bustle the big fellow along."

"Is the *bruja* staying away?" Paul asked. The Villas looked shocked at his mention of a witch, and Paul sensed their reaction. He turned and said, "The lady, she was always missing money. She was always accusing us, the poor devils who worked there, of robbing her. Turned out her little girl was stealing the money. But we had quite a hassle for a long time."

"Elena stays away most of the time," Abel added. "Her brother is much easier to deal with."

"So," Paul said, "someday Carmen and I will stop by for jelly donuts, Abel. Those were always my favorites."

Carmen and Paul walked out together, getting into the pickup. It was their second date. They had seen *Up*, the animated movie, and that was fun. This was good too. Carmen was proud of Paul—how friendly and social he was. She could see the Villas' early misgivings fading away as they got to know him.

When Paul got behind the wheel, he turned to Carmen. "Want to go right home? Or should we sneak somewhere else for an hour?"

The thought of spending more time with Paul Morales was very appealing to

Carmen. She had told her parents she'd be home in the late afternoon. So they had plenty of time. "Let's live dangerously," Carmen answered.

"You got it, doll," Paul replied happily, backing out of the driveway.

They drove over to the beach, where there was a big surf. They got out of the truck and stood on a bluff watching the waves crashing on the rocks.

"Awesome huh?" Paul asked. "I like the sound of the big waves. Sounds like the cymbals in a rock band. I love the loud, clashing noise. You ever go to a rock concert and wallow around in the mosh pit, babe?"

Carmen laughed. "I like rock music. But so far I've steered clear of the mosh pit."

Paul shook his head. "Man, I love the power of the ocean. The waves, they're just incredible."

"You didn't grow up around here, did you, Paul?" Carmen asked.

"What makes you say that?" Paul responded.

"I don't know. I just have a feeling," Carmen said.

"You're right," he said. "I grew up near LA. In the San Fernando Valley. Not the good part. The bad part."

"What made your family move down here, Paul?" she probed. "My friend Ernie, they moved down from LA because his dad got a teaching job at Chavez High. Did your family—"

"There was no family, babe," Paul cut into her question.

Carmen turned and looked at him. "No family?" she repeated. It sounded so sad, so forlorn.

"But, like I said, I got awesome friends," Paul went on, in a chipper tone. "Beto and Abel and Cruz. And, hey, the other day I met a babe at Hortencia's who's so beautiful that the seagulls swoop down for a better look. See them?" He pointed. "They're flying low. They want to see you better, doll. They're talking to each other in seagull talk. They're saying, 'Check out the chick in the yellow pullover,' "

Carmen laughed. She was touched by his compliment. But she got the distinct feeling that he didn't want to answer any more personal questions. That worried Carmen. She liked him. She could imagine eventually loving him, as Naomi loved Ernesto, or like Abel was beginning to love Claudia—if he didn't already. But the blank pages in Paul's book worried Carmen.

Who was he really? Where did he come from? What had happened to his family? Was he running and hiding from some terrible secret? Did he leave Los Angeles to escape a dark past?

Carmen wanted to know the truth, whatever it was, because the worst thing of all was not knowing. Her imagination filled in the blank spaces, and Carmen didn't want to go there. She already cared too much for Paul Morales.

"Look at the gulls!" Paul cried. "I like to hear them screaming. I guess I like all the birds, even the old crows that nobody likes in the *barrio*. They sit on the telephone wires and screech at each other. I wonder what they're saying? They have different sounds, have you noticed? Sometimes it's a harsh 'caw,' but sometimes they make different calls. It must be something to be a bird, to just take off and go far up there in the sky . . ."

"Yeah," Carmen agreed. But she wasn't thinking about birds.

As they walked back to the truck, Paul stopped and looked at Carmen. She stopped too. "I really like those big brown eyes . . .," he told her.

Carmen smiled. When he reached for her hand, she gave it to him. They walked up the rocky path like that.

"You know," Paul remarked, "I really respect Abel that he's going to be able to do something that he's excited about. That's a beef I have with my homies, Beto and Cruz.

111

They work in construction, but they have no real skills. They do hard, dirty work. I'm after them to go to tech school and learn a real skill. That's why I'm trying to learn about film. Maybe I'll just work on the sidelines or something, but I want to know something."

Carmen felt as though she should make a comment, but she wasn't sure what to say. "I don't know, maybe I'll end up being a nurse like my sister wants to be. Or maybe a doctor."

"You got the personality for it, doll," Paul assured her. "You're strong, but you're nice. And pretty too. That helps. Your sister, she's pretty too, but it's a different kind of pretty. I don't think I'd get along with your sister too good. She's like judgmental, right? She's that way, isn't she?"

"Kinda," Carmen admitted. He must have sensed that Lourdes didn't like him. Of course he did. Anybody could see that. Lourdes looked at him as she would look at a cockroach. Paul was the thing that suddenly appeared in the middle of her clean kitchen floor.

"I can see your sister down there at the hospital," he went on. "They bring in a drunk who fell down in the street and cracked his head open. She's taking care of him. But all the time she's saying, 'Hey, you shouldn't be drinking dude. You shouldn't be falling down and hurting yourself and being down here in emergency. It's too crowded already. What's with you anyway?' She's saying, 'Nice, normal people don't do stuff like this. You gotta straighten up and fly right, man.'"

Carmen giggled, nodding her head in agreement. "I can hear her saying that too. Lourdes has little patience with people who break the rules."

They chatted a little more as Paul drove to the Ibarras' home. Then the pickup pulled into the driveway of the house on Nuthatch Lane. Emilio Ibarra just happened to be outside in the front yard. He was examining the drought-resistant succulents that Conchita

113

had just planted. Everyone was being encouraged to stop planting lawns that needed water all the time. Instead, they were supposed to fill their yards with native plants that did well without rain.

When the small pickup pulled in, Mr. Ibarra turned and smiled. Carmen thought to herself, "Did Papa want to make it seem as if he had not been out here for a good long time? Oh, he just popped out coincidentally when I happened to arrive home, did he? Well, it *is* a little late to be returning from a meal that was served around noon."

"So," Emilio Ibarra asked, "did Abel do well as usual?"

"It was wonderful, Papa," Carmen told him. "So delicious! He's a magician in the kitchen."

"Hey Mr. Ibarra," Paul said. "Nice seeing you again. Carmen told me what you've been doing for the veterans. That is way cool, dude . . . er, *sir*."

Paul scrambled back into his truck and drove away.

As the truck disappeared around the corner, Mr. Ibarra turned to his young daughter. "So *mi hija*, you have been gone a good long time with this fellow. What did you find out about his family, his background? I'm sure you had much time to talk, yes?"

"Uh, he didn't say much, Papa," Carmen replied. "He said I have a real nice family. He likes you and Mom and . . . Bernie. He really likes our family."

"That's very well and good that he likes our family, *mi hija*," Mr. Ibarra stated, unsmiling. "But I can see, Carmen, that you are liking this boy more every day that goes by. So . . . it is most important that we learn about his family and his background."

"He doesn't seem to want to talk about that stuff," Carmen offered.

"That stuff?" Mr. Ibarra repeated sharply. "Well, please give all due respect to this young man who you are liking more with every hour that passes. *This stuff* is very important to a father who loves you very much. To a father who does not want any nasty surprises to come popping out of the dark places. Paul is handsome and well-spoken. He is even—I must admit—clever. He knows what to say and what not to say. He is very street-smart."

Mr. Ibarra lifted his right hand in a slow, chopping motion. "But, *mi hija*, these things happen very fast. As a father, I have the right to know what my daughter is getting into. You are only seventeen years old, and, unlike that boy, you are not street-smart. You take everything as it appears. You don't want to look into the shadows and find out if something is moving there."

"Papa, Paul will tell me in his own time," Carmen said, with finality in her tone.

"The next thing I'll hear from your lips is that you love this boy," Mr. Ibarra groaned. "Oh yes. I'm preparing for that. You'll sigh deeply and tell me you are in love with Paul Morales."

"Oh, we're a long way from that," Carmen replied quickly. But the thought of being in love with Paul had crossed her mind. "Papa, he did say that he has no family. He did say that."

"He has no family?" Mr. Ibarra gasped. His eyebrows went up, and his mustache quivered violently. His reaction became theatrical and sarcastic. His head swiveled, and his bulging eyes ranged left and right. It was as if he was trying to figure out an impossible problem. "How, then, did he come into this world? Did he rise out of a pumpkin patch one fine day? *We all have families*. We may lose our families through tragedy or by choice, but everyone has a family. Carmen, does this not alarm you in the least that this boy tells you he has no family? Are you not concerned that he fails to explain that incredible statement?"

"I guess maybe he was an orphan or something," Carmen answered limply.

Lourdes came out of the house. She was the last person Carmen wanted to see at this moment. If she joined in the conversation, she would side with Papa and just make matters worse.

"Carmen," Lourdes said in a harsh voice, "I asked around. Some of my friends have younger sisters who were at Chavez when Paul Morales went there last year. They said he got very uptight when anybody asked him anything personal. He got almost hostile."

Emilio Ibarra's mustache was now in constant motion. "Carmen," he commanded, "do you hear what your sister is saying? You are walking down a dark road without lights. You are captivated by a handsome face and a glib tongue. I want to know *who this boy is*, and I want to know it soon!"

CHAPTER SEVEN

Carmen had ridden several times in Paul Morales's small pickup truck. But he'd never driven with her in her red convertible. On Monday afternoon, when Paul got off work at the computer store at four, Carmen picked him up. His truck was getting an oil change, and she had offered to take him home. They didn't have much time. Carmen had told her father she'd be home by six. But they had time to go to the ice cream store on Tremayne. The butterscotch sundaes were on sale.

Carmen kept thinking about what her father had said. He wanted to know more about Paul Morales to feel comfortable with Carmen dating him. So Carmen was trying to think of a clever way to get Paul to open up. She didn't want to nag him, but she had to find out something to calm her father down.

As Carmen drove toward the ice cream store, Paul said, "You know, doll, I got a real soft spot for this car. If it wasn't for this red convertible, I never would have noticed the hot babe behind the wheel."

"Oh Paul," Carmen laughed.

When Carmen stopped for a red light, she saw Yvette Ozono crossing the street. Yvette was strolling along the sidewalk, looking into the windows of stores listlessly.

"That's Yvette Ozono," Carmen said. "She's the girl who dropped out of school. She's had a lot of troubles. Ernesto's father got her to come back to Chavez. Now she's doing great in math."

"She doesn't look too happy right now," Paul noted. "Look at how her shoulders are slumping. She looks like she's got the weight of the world on her."

"Yeah, you're right," Carmen agreed. "You know, her math teacher, Mr. Cabral, took Yvette and a couple other good math students to a competition in Los Angeles. Maybe they didn't do too well. Maybe Yvette didn't perform like she hoped. I think maybe she needs some cheering up. I'm gonna pull over, Paul."

"Fine," Paul said. "Why don't you invite her to come have a sundae with us? There's nothing like a sundae to perk up your spirits."

"Thanks, Paul. Thanks for suggesting that," Carmen told him, getting out of the car. She stopped before she was fully out and added, "You're so sweet, Paul."

"A compliment that I rarely get," Paul replied with a wry smile. "It's your influence, doll. You bring out the best in me, though it's very deeply buried."

"Hi Yvette," Carmen called to the girl. "How're you doing? I haven't seen you since you came back from the weekend competition. How did it go?"

Yvette turned and looked at Carmen. She had clearly been crying. Carmen was alarmed. Maybe Yvette got nervous during the competition and blew the whole thing. Maybe she felt terrible that she let down Mr. Cabral and the whole team. Maybe she'd made Cesar Chavez High School look lame. The students had gone off in high spirits, expecting to take one of the three top places.

"Oh, it was good," Yvette responded. "I kinda did better than I expected. Me and this guy, Phil Serra, we were the top ones. Mr. Cabral said we were the reason Chavez did so good." What she was saying should have made her ecstatic. But Yvette sounded devastated. Carmen didn't get it.

"Well, congratulations, Yvette. Where did Chavez finish?" Carmen asked.

"We won. We got the trophy. We beat everybody else," Yvette answered.

"Oh wow, that's amazing!" Carmen cried. "I bet Mr. Cabral freaked out!"

"Yeah, he was happy," Yvette said. She seemed so deeply depressed. Carmen would have thought she'd be on cloud nine.

"Yvette, you don't look like a girl who just helped her school win a big math prize," Carmen observed. "What's up? Is something wrong at home?"

"No," Yvette said.

"Yvette, me and Paul are going to get butterscotch sundaes. Why don't you come along?" Carmen suggested.

Yvette glanced at the handsome young man in the convertible. She knew he was Carmen's exciting new boyfriend. He was the guy she was talking about every day at lunch. "Oh, I don't want to spoil it for you guys," Yvette objected. "I'd just be a downer for you. You guys just go ahead and have fun."

"Listen, girl," Paul insisted. "You get in this car and do it *now*. Carmen is talk-ing a mile a minute, and she's giving me a headache. I need somebody else to bal-ance things out. You know how this chick can talk. If you came along, you could maybe calm her down. So get in."

Paul's gesture touched Carmen. Actually, Carmen wasn't talking very much at all this afternoon. Paul just said that to make Yvette feel welcome to join them. Paul knew that Yvette needed somebody right now, and she needed somebody bad. Carmen was blown away that he was that sensitive.

"You sure I wouldn't be ruining it for you guys?" Yvette asked.

"Get in, girl," Paul told her, "unless you're afraid to ride in a car with this chick at the wheel. I'm telling you, it's like riding on a roller coaster. You put a redheaded babe at the wheel of a red convertible, and you're playing with fire."

Yvette smiled a little and got into the backseat. They drove to the ice cream store, and the three of them found a booth in the back.

"So Yvette, what's got you down in the dumps? You can tell us," Carmen asked. "It'll be our secret."

"Yeah," Paul added. "We won't tell anybody. We won't tweet. We won't blab on Facebook."

After taking a spoonful of her butterscotch sundae, Yvette started talking. "Mr. Cabral drove the four of us to the math competition on Saturday. There was me and Phil Serra, and two girls who're in our class. But I don't know them well. Cindy and Margot. You've seen Phil, Carmen. He's in Ms. Hunt's English class. He's smart."

"Yeah, I've seen him," Carmen acknowledged. "Nice guy."

"Well, on the drive back," Yvette continued, "I was all happy about us winning and stuff. Phil was happy too. Me and Phil got to talking. He said he kinda liked me. I was amazed. I mean, I haven't had a boyfriend since Tommy."

Yvette glanced at Paul Morales and explained. "I dated this horrible gangbanger, Coyote. Then I got some sense and left him. I met Tommy Alvarado and went

125

with him. Coyote got jealous and . . . killed Tommy. Since then, I haven't dated at all. I didn't think any boy would like me again. Phil is a nice boy from a nice family. I figured if he knew the truth about me, he'd never date me."

Yvette toyed with her sundae. "Some of the boys at school said I was tainted. I shouldn't be going out with a nice boy 'cause I'm a loser. And it's true. I did lot of bad things when I was with Coyote. I come from a crummy family without no dad. So I told Phil I couldn't go out with him. I felt so bad. I mean, I was so happy and excited. But I knew the boys were right. Phil Serra is good person. He deserves a good girl, not someone like me."

Paul Morales had stopped eating. He looked right at Yvette and reached over. He gently took her chin between his fingers, making her look at him. "Yvette, you're doomed, right? You're the lost . . . the hopeless, right?"

"Yeah," Yvette nodded. "I'm no good . . ."

"Yvette, listen up," Paul commanded. "Lot of us're lost ones out there. You say your dad is missing? So's mine. I don't even know who my dad was. If I ran into the dude tomorrow, I wouldn't know him. And he wouldn't know me. My mom was on crack cocaine, and she never got to see her thirtieth birthday. The County of Los Angeles became my parent, Yvette, and they tried their best to get rid of me. They farmed me out to foster homes, and they tried to get me adopted. But nobody wanted me. People took one look at this grungy little nine-year-old punk. Then they looked for a better kid. They wanted a cute little baby without bad habits. It wasn't me."

Yvette was staring wide-eyed at Paul. "I went from foster home to foster home," Paul went on. "And they were all glad to be rid of me. I was no boy scout during those days I was growing up, girl. Every cop in the neighborhood knew me. I stole. I lied. I cheated. You say you did bad things,

Yvette. I did bad things too. It comes with the territory."

Carmen was shocked at Paul's revelation.

"But listen, girl," he continued, "we didn't neither of us ask for where we were. We didn't ask for the families we were born into. You didn't and I didn't. I'd of liked to be born into a family with a daddy like Emilio Zapata Ibarra. Oh yeah. I'd of liked a mama like Conchita. I'd of liked a family like that Ernesto Sandoval has. Everybody says he's Mr. Perfect. Yeah. His father's a teacher, and that's wonderful. I coulda handled that. It woulda worked for us, huh girl? We woulda liked that setup when we were growin' up. But we got skunked."

Paul was on a roll. "But you know what, Yvette?" he persisted. "We're as good as anybody else. We're better than most of them who came from good homes. We survived all that without turning into monsters. You're a pretty, sweet girl with a good mind. You're doing great. You're not bitter.

I'm a little bitter sometimes, but I haven't let it twist me out of shape. I got cheated out of a good beginning, Yvette. So did you."

Paul's eyes were glowing. His voice was impassioned. He leaned forward toward Yvette. "But that don't mean we can't build a great life. It don't mean we can't have friends who care about us and somebody to love too. I got a chick right here, Carmen, and she's real classy. But I'm not wasting my time thinking I'm not good enough for her. *I am good enough.* And *you're good enough* for that dude who wanted to take you out. Those boys who tore you down, Yvette, they're the ones with the problems, not you."

Carmen sat there stunned for a moment. Then she reached over and put her arm around Paul's shoulders. She was close enough to kiss his cheek, and she did. He needed a shave, but it was still a great kiss. She wanted to kiss him now more than ever.

"Paul," Yvette stammered, "I thought I was the only one as low . . ."

"*Chica*," Paul interrupted her, "the world is full of us—the lost. But just because we come out of dark places don't mean we can't shine like the stars. So, next time you see that dude, Phil Serra, you walk up to him with your head held high. You tell him you've thought it over. And heck yeah, you'd like to go out with him. You have the time of your life with the dude, girl. And don't look back. Don't ever look back. People who're looking back all the time fall into holes. When you look ahead, you see beautiful things like the sun rising."

The despair seemed to drain out of Yvette's face. Touched and speechless, she dug into her butterscotch sundae and ate every bite of it. In a few minutes they were talking about the math competition. The kids from West Los Angeles had gotten pretty upset. Yvette, a kid from the *barrio*, had put up so many points that it was a landslide for Chavez.

Carmen drove Yvette home to Starling Street. As they got out of the car, Yvette hugged Carmen and Paul. Then she ran into the apartment she shared with her mother and siblings. Back behind the wheel of the convertible, Carmen said, "That was so beautiful, Paul. I was never so proud of anyone as I was of you. You changed Yvette's life. With those words you gave her hope again. Do you realize what a wonderful thing you did?"

"Hey babe, all I did was tell the truth," Paul demurred. He nodded his head and looked away from Carmen.

Then Carmen took Paul home to his apartment on Cardinal Street. When they got to the parking lot, he asked, "Wanna see my room, doll?"

"I'd love to see it," Carmen replied.

Paul led Carmen around the back of a large apartment building to stairs leading up to a blue door. Paul unlocked the door to his tiny studio apartment. The one room was a combination bedroom, living room, and small kitchen. The tiny bathroom was the only other room. The place was messy but not dirty.

"It's real easy to clean," Paul demonstrated. "Just stand in the middle with a broom and swish it around. Presto, housecleaning over!"

Books and newspapers were stacked on the sofa and floor. They were spilling over a little end table. "The sofa gets to be a bed, see," Paul explained. "But first I gotta get all the junk off it, and that's too much trouble sometimes. So I crash in my sleeping bag on the floor. This is what a guy gets for the cheap rent I pay."

Paul then pointed over to the kitchen area, where cups of noodles were everywhere. "Wonderful invention," Paul commented. "Just heat some water, pour it in the cup to the rim here, stir it up. *Voilá!* Dinner is served. Costs less than fifty cents."

"I like that stuff too," Carmen laughed.

Paul turned serious then. "You know, doll, I dropped a lot of heavy stuff on you and Yvette, didn't I? I got carried away trying to encourage her. Maybe you heard a lot of stuff you weren't ready for. I probably shocked you, girl."

"Yeah, you did," Carmen admitted.

"And?" Paul Morales asked. "Where do we go from here?"

Carmen came face to face with Paul and put her hands on his shoulders. She stood tiptoe and brought him down to where she could kiss him. That was the only answer she could give him. And that was the only answer he wanted.

When Carmen got home, her father was working on the computer. The city council was going to vote on a lot of programs next week. He was preparing his presentations. The budget was due, for one thing. They were setting up seminars to help people avoid foreclosures on their homes. And they were also trying to keep from laying off police officers and firefighters. But when Carmen came in, Mr. Ibarra stopped working and looked at her. "So, how was your day, *mi hija*?"

Carmen looked at her father and thought how proud she was of this good man. She remembered Paul's bitter comment that he wished he'd been born into a family like hers. "I love you, Papa," Carmen told her dad. "I think I'll make us coffee so we can talk."

"That would be nice," Mr. Ibarra replied, looking at his daughter intently. He sensed that she had something very important to say.

In a few minutes, Carmen reappeared with two cups of coffee and sat down on the sofa. Her father came and sat beside her. "Is the coffee okay, Papa?" she inquired.

"Ahhh, *perfecto*," he remarked, "just the right amount of sugar and cream."

"Papa," she began, "you wanted to know who Paul Morales was. This afternoon he told me. He didn't mean to tell me. There was this girl who was feeling so sad and unworthy because she comes from a troubled background. And to help her feel better about herself, Paul shared his story."

Emilio Ibarra's mustache twitched a little. He took a long swallow of coffee. He looked at Carmen and waited.

"Paul doesn't know who his father was," Carmen explained. "He was absent from the family. Paul's mother was very sick. She used drugs, and she died when Paul was nine years old. He was taken by the county and put in foster homes. They tried to adopt him out, but most people prefer babies. So nobody ever wanted him. Paul said he was a rough little boy."

Carmen had decided to leave out the details of all the trouble he had gotten into. Papa didn't have to know how well the local police knew him. She didn't want to share everything he told Yvette. "Anyway, when you get to be an adult in the foster care system, they just sort of cut you loose. So Paul was on his own."

135

"Well," Mr. Ibarra commented, "that is a tragic story indeed. The boy is to be commended that he overcame all of that to graduate from high school and now to be in college."

There was genuine sadness on the man's face. He leaned back on the sofa and closed his eyes for a moment. He looked conflicted. He was by nature a compassionate man. He was always reaching out to people in trouble. He was especially concerned for the young. Carmen remembered many times when he reached out to youths who were recovering drug addicts.

But this situation involved his daughter, someone he loved very much. Yes, this young man was making a life, despite all the hardships. Part of Emilio Ibarra respected Paul Morales for what he had overcome. Part of him wondered whether the boy was damaged by his terrible experiences. And how would that impact Carmen?

"Paul told me he would have liked to be born in our family," Carmen offered. "He would have liked a father like you and a mother like Mama. He said that would have been wonderful."

Carmen waited a moment to make sure Papa was listening. "Paul said he comes from a dark place. But that doesn't mean he can't shine as brightly as anybody else. That's why he's so ambitious. He's taking that filmmaking class and stuff. Papa, I think he's pretty wonderful. I know this is hard to hear. But I don't think I ever met a boy I admired more than Paul Morales."

"It's very good that Paul hasn't allowed his past to destroy his dreams," her father finally said. "*Mi hija*, we must invite him to a party at our house so we can all get to know him better. Lourdes is giving a party for Ivan. It's Ivan's twenty-first birthday. It will be a nice party here at the house, and Paul must come to help us celebrate."

CHAPTER EIGHT

At school on Thursday, Carmen got her history test back from Luis Sandoval. She'd gotten an A, and she was excited about her grade. But she was even more excited about what she was doing that night. She and Paul were going to a small theater downtown to see the short-subject films his community college class had produced. Paul had a film showing, which was part animation and part live action. He seemed eager for Carmen to see it.

That day at lunch, Carmen, Naomi, and Tessie were eating with Yvette. Then Mira Nuñez walked over to them. After Naomi Martinez had ended her relationship with Clay, he started taking Mira out. Carmen and Naomi both believed Clay didn't really like Mira. He was just using the girl to try to make Naomi jealous. Clay wanted Naomi back. But he was beginning to fear she wouldn't come back. Naomi and Ernesto Sandoval were growing closer every day. Mira sensed that Clay Aguirre did not care about her as much as she cared for him. But she was hopeful.

"Hey Naomi," Mira said in a forlorn voice. "You were with Clay a long time. You guys must have had some chemistry going. I don't know how to get through to Clay. I want us to be, you know, more in touch with each other. You got any advice, Naomi?"

Carmen could see that Naomi didn't know what to say. Naomi had liked Clay since middle school. Their relationship had just very slowly evolved into something deeper. Mira was trying to build something with Clay. But he was still hung up on his old girlfriend, Naomi.

"I don't know, Mira," Naomi finally replied. "Just give it time."

Mira looked at Carmen then. "Clay is really ticked off at you, Carmen. He blames you for telling Naomi to dump him when they had that fight."

Mira turned her attention back to Naomi. "Clay said you're too weak to have broken from him. But Carmen gave you the guts to do it, Naomi."

"I supported Naomi's decision," Carmen admitted. "But she made up her own mind. Naomi isn't as weak as Clay thinks. She just takes longer to get fired up. Look, Mira, Clay hit Naomi. That was a deal breaker, right? I mean, come on, Mira, would you stand for that?"

"Clay is kinda rude to me sometimes," Mira confessed, "but he's never hit me. I'm telling you something, Carmen. Clay told me he'd like to make trouble for you and your boyfriend, that guy Paul. He says he's hurting a lot over losing Naomi. He wants you to be hurting too. He wants you to pay for telling Naomi to dump him."

"Another of Clay's good qualities," Carmen pointed out. "He's paranoid and vindictive. Mira, you sure you *want* this dude?"

"I'm kinda into him," Mira admitted. "I heard a guy on TV say that love can be an addiction. I guess I'm addicted to Clay."

But Mira wasn't going to be put off track. She was going to tell Carmen what she had to say. "Anyway, the other day we were out driving, and he spotted Paul in his truck. Clay got real excited. He said maybe Paul has another girlfriend, and he's going to see her. He was really hoping for that. So he followed Paul. I was bummed out, Carmen. We followed Paul for miles. Clay just wouldn't give up. He was absolutely sure Paul would pull into some driveway. Then a pretty chick would come running out and fling herself into his arms. Boy, did he want to bring you news of that. He even had his phone ready to take pictures."

Naomi lay on her back on the grass eating an apple. She shook her head in disgust.

141

"Mira, *run*," she advised. "I shoulda done that years ago. What kind of an idiot was I to stick with Clay?"

Carmen, Tessie, and Yvette all laughed.

"But then Paul, he pulls into the prison," Mira went on. "The men's prison."

Carmen blinked. "What prison?" she asked.

"You know, the big one in South Bay," Mira said, feeling glad she finally had Carmen's attention. "He drove down the long driveway, got to the gate, and was put through. Clay was furious. Clay, he said some of Paul's lowlife friends must be locked up there, and he's going to visit them. Clay lost interest then, and we went to eat."

Mira must have thought the rest of her tale was important. So she continued. "We got greasy hamburgers at some joint he likes. I like fish tacos, but we never get any. It's Clay's way or the highway."

"*Run*, girl," Naomi repeated herself. Mira shrugged and walked away. Carmen was left to wonder whether Paul did have friends in prison. It wouldn't be impossible. He had told Yvette and her about a troubled past. He was the kind of a guy who wouldn't turn away from a friend who was locked up. It would be like Paul Morales to try to help the friend through it all.

Paul never mentioned having a friend in prison, though. Then again, he probably left a lot of things out, Carmen thought.

Paul came to the Ibarra house at six thirty to pick up Carmen. Her parents were very cordial to him. Carmen believed Paul wouldn't mind her telling Mama and Papa about his history. But she had asked them not to say anything. She just didn't want to embarrass him. If she and Paul grew closer, she was sure he'd tell her parents about himself when he was ready.

"So, you've made a movie, eh?" Mr. Ibarra inquired.

"Yeah, just a short one," Paul replied. "The technology has made it so easy now.

But during those few minutes, you gotta pack in something that grabs the viewer."

Darkness was settling in earlier during the winter months. By the time they reached the theater, the sky was dark, and a crescent moon hung in the sky. Paul's teacher, a lovely Asian woman, Anisa Lee, greeted him. Her black hair hung down her back in a long pony tail.

Paul introduced Carmen to Anisa Lee. Then they sat down to wait for the movies to come on. Most of the people in the theater were Paul's fellow students in the film class, along with their families or friends. Paul's film was the third one to be screened. Carmen didn't know much about filmmaking, but she really wanted to like what Paul had done.

Paul's film started with several dogs in computer animation. There were some terriers, a bulldog, and a collie. There was also a litter of darling golden retriever puppies. All of the dogs were in cages in a building that looked like the animal shelter.

Human actors appeared then. Carmen recognized Abel and Claudia, Beto and Cruz. They all wore makeup to look much older than they were. They must have all volunteered to be in Paul's film. The four people seemed to be looking into the cages at the animals. They hurried past the collie, the terriers, and the bulldogs. They stopped by the cage filled with the golden retriever puppies.

In another few seconds, the animation resumed. The bulldog rested his chin on his paws. He appeared to be weeping. The collie's ears drooped. The terriers had stopped wagging their tails. Now they stared blankly at the bars of their cage.

The four actors reappeared. You could see only their backs as they walked out of the animal shelter. They were laughing and chattering. You could hear the happy yips of the dogs that had been chosen.

The camera returned to the last cage, the one that had held the golden retriever puppies. It was empty. The film then ended abruptly. The puppies had been chosen, and they were being taken to a happy future. The other dogs had been rejected. They would always be rejected.

The title of Paul's film was *The Lost*.

There was a lot of applause when the film ended. The audience applauded for all the short films, but they seemed to applaud a bit more for Paul's film.

Carmen felt a lump in her throat. She knew the film was not just about dogs at the animal shelter. It wasn't only about the older dogs never getting a home while the cute puppies were snatched up. The film was about a little boy in Los Angeles. It was about a nine-year-old who waited in vain to be adopted. It was about the scars he bore. The film was not saying that people are evil or uncaring. The point was that people preferred to adopt a baby or a very young child. They didn't want to take a chance on a nine-year-old kid "with issues."

"Well?" Paul asked Carmen as they left the theater. "Waddya think?"

"Paul, that blew me away!" Carmen gasped. "It was so sad, but you made it all seem so real. I don't know that much about filmmaking, but it touched my heart. Paul, it's a . . . a work of art. And I couldn't believe Abel and Claudia and your homies were in it."

"Yeah, when you can't afford to hire actors, you impose on your friends," Paul explained. "What can I say?"

"Which of the dogs was you, Paul?" Carmen asked.

Paul laughed. "The bulldog."

"What did your teacher say about the film?" Carmen inquired.

"Anisa liked it," Paul with happiness in his voice. "She gave me an A. Now all the films'll be entered in a countywide competition. The four best will get cash prizes. And then the winners get to go to the Sundance Film Festival and see how the pros do it."

"Paul!" Carmen cried. "This is so exciting! I'm so happy for you."

"Hey, doll!" Paul put up his hands, palms facing her. "It's a long road to the festival."

As they walked to the truck, they talked more about the film and Paul's chances of winning. Then they headed for Hortencia's for *churros* and hot chocolate. They were driving for about ten minutes when the pleasant conversation stopped. Paul's face hardened, his eyes narrowing. "What the devil is going on?" he almost shouted.

Carmen turned to see an old green van stopped at the side of the road. Three police cars were on the scene, all with their red lights pulsating in the darkness. Two guys in baggy clothing were standing near the van, their hands cuffed behind their backs.

"That's Beto and Cruz!" Paul cried, slamming on the brakes and parking near the police action. "They didn't do anything! Why did the cops handcuff them? Why are they getting hassled when they didn't do anything!"

Paul reached for the door handle to get out of the cab.

"Paul, don't get involved," Carmen cried. "Don't get mixed up in it!"

Paul turned to Carmen, a harsh look on his face. "This isn't right!" he snapped.

"Paul, please," Carmen begged him. "Don't get involved. They'll arrest you too. The police don't just stop a car for no reason and handcuff guys!"

"Doll, you've led a very sheltered life," Paul snapped. "The cops hassle guys in baggy clothes and shaved heads for doing nothing. The cops just assume they're gangbangers who're up to something. I know those dudes, and they didn't do anything!"

One of the police officers glanced in Paul's direction as he got out of the cab of the truck. "There's nothing to see here, sir," the officer commanded. "Please get back in your truck and leave."

"These guys are my friends," Paul responded. "They didn't do anything wrong. Why are they being arrested?"

Another police officer joined the one who had ordered Paul to leave. They both came walking toward Paul. Carmen's heart was beating so fast she thought it would burst through her chest. It was surreal. She'd never been involved in anything like this.

"Do you have your driver's license and registration, sir?" one of the officers asked.

Paul pulled out his ID and handed it to the officer. "Can't you just tell me what's going on here?"

The other officer came to the cab of the pickup truck. He looked at Carmen and said, "Miss, would you step out of the truck, please?"

Carmen's legs were shaking badly. She thought she would fall on her face when she was out of the cab. But she complied.

"Do you have ID, miss?" the officer asked.

Carmen handed him her driver's license and ID from Cesar Chavez High School. The officer shone his flashlight around the inside of the cab. Then he handed Carmen back her ID. Paul got his ID back too, but not before the officer had gone to the police car and checked him out.

"All right, Mr. Morales," the officer told him, "please return to your truck. You and the young lady go to wherever you were going."

"What did those guys do?" Paul asked again. "They're my best friends, and I want to know what's happening."

"Mr. Morales, you could be arrested for interfering with a police investigation. You better leave now," the officer advised with a hard edge to his voice.

Paul got back into the truck. Carmen sat numbly beside him. Paul let out a stream of the ugliest language Carmen had ever heard. He started the truck and drove slowly down the street.

"I'm going around the block. I'm coming back here and see what's happening to my homies," Paul declared. "I'm not going to Hortencia's and having a *churro* while my friends are getting busted for nothing!"

"Please Paul," Carmen pleaded, "let's just get out of here."

Paul circled the block and returned to where Beto and Cruz had been in handcuffs. The two boys were standing by the green van, their hands free. One police car remained. The officer inside it seemed to be making out a report. Paul cruised alongside the green van.

"Hey dudes, what was that all about?" Paul called out.

"The genius here," Beto explained, laughing as he pointed to Cruz. "He forgot to get the new tags put on the license plate."

"I got the tags home somewhere," Cruz protested. "I lost it in all the junk in my room. All that over a lousy little sticker the size of a postage stamp!"

"But why did they handcuff you?" Carmen asked.

Beto looked at Carmen and smiled patronizingly. "Your chick doesn't know the rules of the road, does she, Paul?"

"No," Paul answered, laughing. "She grew up in Disneyland, and stuff like this never happens there." The tension had gone from Paul's face. He spoke to Carmen with a smirk. "See, babe, cops think you're a gangbanger if you dress like one and shave your head like these fools do. So when they pull you over for any reason, they don't take chances. Beto, Cruz, listen up. Go down to the thrift store and get some decent jeans. Let your stupid hair grow." The three boys laughed.

Then Paul and Carmen finally continued their drive to Hortencia's. The lone police officer still sat in his cruiser, making out his report.

"Cruz and Beto, they never committed a crime, babe," Paul explained. "I mean something they were booked for. Yeah, they boosted liquor from a delivery truck a coupla times, but that was ages ago. They're really working stiffs. They live on a real paycheck like the rest of us. Believe it or not, they live at home. They can't afford

153

their own places yet. Cruz's eighteen, and Beto is almost nineteen."

"Paul! You scared the life out of me!" Carmen screamed at him, slapping him hard on the chest. "I was terrified! I thought we'd all be arrested! Imagine my papa getting a call to come bail his daughter out of jail." Carmen's whole body was trembling.

Paul looked at Carmen. "You *are* shaking, doll."

He went to put his arm around Carmen, but she shook him off. She scooted away from him on the seat. Paul realized he'd messed up.

"Baby, I'm sorry," he told her softly. "It's just that I get really fired up when I see my friends getting' hassled. I can't just walk away. That's how I am."

On the other side of the truck's cab, Carmen only sniffed and dabbed her nose with a tissue.

Paul tried to lighten things up. "Hey girl, I bet you never thought dating Paul

Morales would get this exciting, did you?" He flashed his biggest smile and waited for a response from Carmen.

"It's not funny!" Carmen protested, still not looking at him.

"Well," Paul sighed, "I'm really sorry, baby. I had no idea you'd be so scared. . . . I'm sorry."

Carmen did not respond.

Paul started driving toward Hortencia's. By the time the truck pulled into the parking lot, Carmen was at least talking with Paul again. Carmen told him that she had no intention of telling her parents about what happened. No way. And he had better not say anything either. That's all Emilio Zapata Ibarra would have to hear.

That was all right with Paul. He felt relieved. If she didn't want her dad to know, then she must be planning on staying his girlfriend. That was good enough for him now, even if she wasn't happy with him.

Carmen thought the evening could not go any farther downhill. But then she spotted Ivan and Lourdes, already eating tamales in Hortencia's.

"Carmen!" Lourdes shouted when she saw her sister come in with Paul. "Over here. You guys come sit with us. There's plenty of room."

"Oh no!," Carmen thought. "*Now* it's the worst thing that could happen." Ivan and Lourdes had been coming down the same street that Paul and Carmen were on. They'd probably seen the green van and the two boys handcuffed. Maybe they recognized them as Paul's friends. Lourdes had seen Cruz and Beto before. Maybe they even saw Paul outside his pickup arguing with the police. And they would go home and tell Mr. Ibarra the whole sordid story. His mustache would jump right off his upper lip.

"Over here!" Lourdes called shrilly.

Carmen had no choice. She and Paul walked over and sat down in the booth. Carmen froze and waited for the worst.

"Hey Lourdes, Ivan," Paul greeted them. Paul wasn't sure of how Ivan was going to respond. Paul had really given Ivan a hard time the last time they talked. But Ivan looked up at Paul and Carmen, and he smiled.

"I'm so excited," Ivan announced. "Lourdes's parents are giving me a birthday party at their house a week from this Friday. I'll be twenty-one years old. Abel Ruiz was kind enough to offer to do some of the food. And this guy Oscar Perez is going to play music. It's not operatic music, but they say it's very good Latino music. It's going to be quite a bash. You have to come, Paul. You will come, won't you?"

"Uh yeah, sure," Paul replied. "Nice of you to invite me, man."

Paul exchanged a look with Carmen. Their worst fears were unfounded. Lourdes and Ivan had not seen the incident with the green van. "So, twenty-one, huh?" Paul inquired. "You're getting up there, man. Next thing you know, Social Security."

Ivan Redondo laughed, his voice cracking. "I swear I *do* feel old sometimes," he admitted.

When Paul and Carmen finished their *churros* and hot chocolate, they went out into the night. They stood next to the pickup and just stared at each other. Finally, Paul spoke.

"I thought our goose was cooked," he declared. "I thought they'd seen *everything,* and they wanted an explanation."

"I could just picture Papa when they told him. I could see his mustache jumping right off his face," Carmen commented. Her tone was still a little cold.

"Yeah," Paul agreed, "I could see his mustache jumping off his face." A second later, he smirked. Then he couldn't help himself. A giggle snorted out of him.

Carmen cracked a smile.

Then they began to laugh so hard that tears streamed down their faces.

CHAPTER NINE

Late that night, Carmen got a text message from Paul. He found her little purse with ladybugs on it in the cab of his truck. In all the excitement last night, she'd let it slip from her handbag. Paul thought Carmen must have left it there. Paul said he could drop it off when he got off work. She texted him back that she'd pick it up on the way to school.

Carmen didn't care about the few dollars in the purse, but it had been a birthday gift from Bernie. So she prized it. On her way to Chavez High on Friday morning, she swung by Cardinal Street to pick it up.

As Carmen slowed down in front of the apartment building, a middle-aged lady hailed her. "You must be Carmen Ibarra," she said. "Paul had to go to work early—they're doing inventory. He said to give you this." She had the little coin purse in her hand.

Carmen parked the convertible and got out. "Thanks so much," she said. "Paul texted me last night that he found it."

"Paul is such a thoughtful young man," the landlady commented. "I've had a lot of trouble renting that tiny studio apartment up those steep stairs. Then those nice boys came along and rented it. Haven't had a bit of trouble since."

Carmen didn't know Paul had a roommate when he rented the studio apartment. He never mentioned having one.

"When did Paul's roommate move out?" Carmen asked.

"Oh, it's been almost a year," the lady responded. "But he wasn't a roommate, dear. It was his brother, David. I was amazed both boys could make do in that small place, but they did. David was older than Paul by a year or two, I suppose."

Carmen stiffened. Paul had a brother? A brother he never mentioned? Carmen thought that omission was really strange. When Paul related the sad story of his absent father and his mother dying young, why didn't he mention his brother? When Paul was nine, David must have been eleven or twelve.

"David was just as nice as Paul," the landlady continued. "No drinking, no loud parties. Not even smoking. So quiet and respectful. You rent to young people these days, and you expect all kinds of problems. But no. When they first moved in, about two years ago, Paul was in Chavez High School. They'd come from Los Angeles. David owned that pickup. It was his car. Paul didn't have anything to drive. He usually rode his bike."

"I wonder why David moved out?" Carmen mused. "I wonder why he'd leave his truck?"

"Oh goodness, I don't know about that," the landlady responded. "I'm not the sort of person who pries into the personal lives of my tenants. It was very sudden, though. Paul never said his brother was moving out. He was just gone one day, and Paul was driving the pickup. I finally asked Paul if he was coming back. You see, I charged the boys a little extra rent since there was two of them in there when those studios are meant for one. Paul told me his brother wasn't coming back. So I lowered the rent."

Carmen felt weird, wondering why Paul didn't talk about his brother. "I suppose David comes to visit sometimes," Carmen said, probing for information.

"No," the landlady responded. "I haven't seen him since. That surprised me, because the boys seemed so close when they lived here. They look so much alike too. Big, strapping boys with that blue-black hair, those beautiful eyes. I always figured David had gone back to Los

Angeles for work or something. Perhaps they had a falling-out. One never knows. Anyway, I'm glad I could give you your little coin purse. It's just darling."

"Thanks a lot," Carmen said, returning to her convertible. Another dark cloud had sailed into her sky. Why hadn't Paul said a word about his brother? Where was his brother? Had something terrible happened to him? Wherever he was, he didn't need his pickup anymore. That was worrying.

Carmen headed for school, but she couldn't get David Morales off her mind.

When Carmen arrived at the campus, she saw Ernesto Sandoval and Abel Ruiz walking to their classes. "Hi guys," she said cheerfully, not showing her anxiety. Ernesto couldn't have known Paul as a student at Chavez since he moved to the *barrio* just recently. But Abel had gotten to know Paul better at the donut shop. Carmen wanted to come right out and ask Abel whether he knew Paul had a brother named

David. But she didn't want it getting back to Paul that she knew. So she tried a roundabout way.

"Paul is really close to those guys, Beto and Cruz. He calls them his *hermanos*. I bet Paul would have liked having a real brother, huh Abel?" Carmen probed.

"I don't know," Abel replied ruefully. "I got this big brother, Tomás. And he's sort of a pain in the neck. So maybe Paul is lucky being an only child."

So, Carmen thought, Abel didn't know about the brother either. He and Paul were pretty good friends, but Abel didn't know. That made Carmen even more concerned.

All that day, Carmen thought of little else but David Morales. What had happened to him? Why did he suddenly disappear?

By the time school ended that day, Carmen had made up her mind. She was beginning to care a lot for Paul Morales. She was thinking about him all the time.

But she had to know whether he had secrets in his life so dark and terrible that they would eventually tear them apart. She had to know.

Carmen sat in her red convertible in the Chavez High parking lot and dialed Paul. "I gotta see you, Paul," she said when he answered.

"Why? What's up?" Paul asked.

"I just need to talk to you. When do you get off work?" Carmen asked.

"Four," he replied. "Are you okay, babe? You sounded weird when you first came on the phone."

"I'll be there at four." Carmen said, matter-of-factly. "Maybe we can go in that little coffee shop next to where you work. We can talk there."

"Sure," he said. "You sure you're okay?"

"Yes," Carmen responded, but she wasn't. She felt worried and sick. Her relationship with Paul was important to her now. She didn't want it to end. She didn't want to keep wondering about a brother who seemed to disappear into thin air.

Paul came out of the computer store at five minutes after four. They walked to the little coffee shop next door and ordered lattes.

"Paul," Carmen began, once the lattes were served, "I got your text message last night about my coin purse. I got it from your landlady this morning. It's, uh . . . special to me 'cause my little sister gave it to me for my birthday."

"That's good," Paul said. "I would have dropped it off, but my boss called last night. Had to go in early. Hey babe, you don't look so good. What's the matter?"

"Your landlady said you had a brother named David who used to live with you," Carmen blurted out. "I just didn't think you had a brother . . ."

"Yeah well," Paul shrugged. "I never said I was an only child, did I?"

He drank a little of his latte. Then he looked right at Carmen. "The less people know about David, the better. That way, I don't have to talk about him. You know, people judge. I was going to tell you eventually but . . ."

Carmen remembered something then. The recollection struck her like a blow. When Clay Aguirre followed Paul's truck, hoping to find Paul visiting another girl, he saw Paul turn into the prison in South Bay. Carmen looked at Paul and asked, "Is he in prison?"

"Yeah," Paul admitted. "How'd you guess?"

Carmen told him what Clay Aguirre had done and what Mira had said he'd seen— Paul driving into the prison.

"David is doing five for a burglary of a store," Paul explained. "He might get out a lot sooner for good behavior. He's doing pretty good, going to school, getting a college education. He's trying to get with the program. I see him every chance I get.

He's the only blood family I got. We had a grandmother, but she died last year."

His dark eyes filled with pain. Carmen reached over and covered his hand with hers. "David," Paul went on, "he was twelve when our mother died. We got sent to different foster homes. It tore us up 'cause we were close. We were closer than most brothers, 'cause we were all we had. Then they even took that away from us."

"David's a good guy," Paul went on. "He just got in with a bad crowd and he wanted stuff more than I did. He had an even rougher time than I did in the system. He got beat up by the older kids in the house. I think if they'd stuck us in the same foster home, we'd of done better. David woulda done better. I'm sorry, babe, that I didn't tell you sooner. But it's not a thing a guy likes to talk about, you know?"

Carmen smiled. "It's okay, Paul. I know you said I grew up in Disneyland, but it's not quite like that. I've been through a lot with my friends. I know what's out there. I can deal with stuff. Now that you've told me, I don't respect you any less. The only thing that would have hurt me was if I'd found out you weren't there for your brother anymore. But I know you well enough to realize that wouldn't happen. You're awfully special, Paul. And I hope you know that you mean a lot to me."

"You're pretty cool, babe," Paul whispered. "I always knew there was a beautiful soul behind those big brown eyes." He took another swallow of latte. "It's okay if you tell your parents about David, Carmen. But don't talk to people at school. I'd hate for some creep like Clay Aguirre to find out and make a circus out of it."

"Yeah," Carmen agreed, putting more sugar in her drink.

"Babe," Paul admitted, "you could do a lot better than me, you know. You're pretty. You're smart. You come from a great family. Man, you're the daughter of a councilman! You could do a lot better than the guy you're drinking lattes with."

"You could do a lot better too, Paul," Carmen countered. "I talk too much. I'm not all that pretty. I'm excitable. I almost had a heart attack when those cops came and asked me to step out of the truck. I worry like crazy about things, and I'm the most terrible cook in the world. And—and this is the worst—I love Duran Duran. I just absolutely love their stuff."

Paul threw back his head and laughed. "Duran Duran? Are those old guys still around?" Then he saw the look on Carmen's face. He thought maybe he had hurt her feelings.

"Well," he said lamely, "I kinda like them too."

They ordered two more lattes. When they were delivered, Paul sang a bad imitation of Duran Duran. "'Dark sun rose on the ridge cut clear across the sky. As good a day as any to die . . .'"

"'Red Carpet Massacre'!" Carmen squealed. "You do know them!"

Paul grinned. "I'm older than you, doll," he said.

Paul and Carmen clicked their coffee cups together and had more of a discussion before they parted. Carmen drove home, a load lifted from her heart. She could deal with most things as long as she knew what she was dealing with. The only things she couldn't handle were mysteries. And one mystery had been solved tonight.

When Carmen came into the house, her father was sitting there with four men and a woman. Carmen didn't recognize any of them. They were drinking coffee and eating cookies that Conchita Ibarra had just made. They were warm from the oven.

"Carmen," Emilio Ibarra announced, "this is the nucleus of the new Nicolo Sena Scholarship fund. Everyone, this is *mi hija*, Carmen."

Mr. Ibarra introduced the businesspeople from the *barrio* who were interested in funding the scholarship program. It had flourished in the *barrio* ten years earlier. It was the scholarship that enabled Luis Sandoval to become a teacher and his brother to become a lawyer. It had been how more than two dozen young men and women rose from poor homes to go to college and become professionals. The city council members promised matching funds.

Sitting in the Ibarra home, as Papa introduced them, were successful businesspeople of the *barrio*. One was the owner of several apartments on Cardinal Street. Another was the owner of the largest supermarket in the *barrio*. A third was the lady who ran four hair and nail salons. Next to her was the manager of the local bank. They would provide the seed money to reestablish the scholarship in time for the current senior class of Cesar Chavez High School to compete for funds for their freshman year in college.

"Oh Papa," Carmen thought but did not say out loud, "that's wonderful. It's really happening. You said if you got elected to the city council, you'd do all these good things. And I believed you, but I didn't think it would all happen so fast. Already we had the veterans' weekend and now this! I'm so proud of you, Papa!" But with all the people in the room, she could only smile at her papa. Emilio Ibarra knew what she was thinking and beamed back at her. Carmen excused herself and left the room. Her father continued conducting his meeting and making plans with the businesspeople.

After they had all left, Carmen found her father sitting alone on the sofa, looking tired. He pressed his fingers into his closed eyes and said, "It has been a long day, but I'm happy. I think this is what I was born to do. All the businesses I have been in, they were good and they took care of my family. But this is what I was meant to do." He smiled and put his arm around

Carmen, hugging her. "I am fulfilled, *mi hija*."

Carmen snuggled beside her father on the sofa, his arm around her shoulders. Sitting with him, she was flooded with good memories. She recalled walks in the park, riding on his shoulders, going out on the bay with him, and seeing how he managed the sails of their rented boat. Carmen always felt safe with him, as if nothing could happen when he was beside her. He made her feel like a princess. Sometimes Emilio Zapata Ibarra wore the plastic sheriff's badge and was very strict and bombastic. He kept the wrong kinds of people out of his house. Even then, in her embarrassment, Carmen knew it was all out of love for her, for her sisters and brother, for their mother.

"Papa," Carmen said, "Paul shared something with me today. I want to tell you about it. He said I should tell you and Mama, but I shouldn't talk about it at school. There's some kids who'd use it against him and against me for liking him."

Mr. Ibarra looked very serious. "Conchita!" he called to his wife in the kitchen. "Come out here and listen to what our daughter wants to tell us."

Conchita Ibarra appeared, drying her hands from cleaning up after making the cookies. She sat down in the little rocker opposite the sofa, and she looked at Carmen with her big, soft eyes. They were darker than Carmen's, brown but a shade darker. They were very beautiful.

"I told you guys that Paul had a very rough childhood," Carmen explained. "I told you all about that, but today he told me it wasn't just him. When his mother died, Paul was nine. He had a brother too who was twelve. Paul never told me about his brother. He never told anybody, I guess. His name is David, and he's three years older than Paul. They were sent to different foster homes. So they didn't grow up together, but they tried to be close."

Mr. Ibarra was listening intently. He sensed some disturbing information was coming.

"David got in with bad friends," Carmen continued, "and he committed a crime. He burglarized a store. He was caught. And they sentenced him to five years in prison. But he could get out sooner if he does real well there. Paul said David's trying to do his best. He's going to school and getting a college education."

"Is he in prison around here?" Mr. Ibarra asked.

"Yes, the place in South Bay," Carmen replied.

"I've been there," Conchita Ibarra said. "The ladies from Our Lady of Guadalupe have a Bible study. We go and pray with the Hispanic boys who are in that prison. There are many of them, and they appreciate every little thing you do for them."

"Well," Carmen continued, "Paul visits his brother a lot. And he wants to help him when he gets out. I respect him that he hasn't turned his back on his brother. He told me to tell you guys because you have the right to know."

All the time Carmen was talking about David Morales, she was looking down at her hands. Now she found the courage to look up at her parents. Her mother looked sad and concerned. Emilio Zapata Ibarra's eyes were wider than Carmen had ever seen them. Carmen couldn't tell whether he was shocked, or angry, or both.

"Carmen . . . Carmen . . ." her father sighed. "This is a difficult thing for me. I understand that there are situations where children are damaged, and they get involved in crime. It's all over the *barrio*. Not just the *barrio* either. The families are not strong, and the children are left to their own devices. I have pity for these boys. I have compassion for Paul and all he had to overcome. Perhaps his brother was not so strong, and he fell under the weight of the parents' faults."

Emilio Ibarra dropped his head for a moment before going on. "But, *mi hija*, I want only the best for you. I would wish for you a life filled with sunshine and no shadows. I would hope for a happy family with merry aunts and uncles . . . good, strong people for your own children to model themselves after. I worry that now there is a brother in prison. I worry for you, *mi hija*."

"Papa, I understand," Carmen said quietly. "But Paul is one of the best, most compassionate, and most decent boys I have ever known. I know in my heart that he's good for me. I know that it was meant that we should meet."

CHAPTER TEN

At six o'clock on the Friday that the Ibarras were hosting the birthday party for Ivan Redondo, the house phone rang. Carmen answered. The party was scheduled to begin at seven. Abel Ruiz had already brought delightful little sandwiches filled with ham, cheese, and *jalapeño* peppers. Conchita Ibarra was icing a beautiful chocolate layer cake.

"Hello?" Carmen said, thinking it was Paul, telling her he was on his way and would soon be arriving. But it wasn't Paul. It was a very upset Ivan Redondo.

"Oh Carmen," he wailed, "this is terrible. This is so awful. I came out, got in my car to come over there, and the car won't start! My parents are gone, and I don't know what to do. I'm so sorry. Of all the times for my car to quit on me! It's almost too late to call a cab and expect to get there on time, Carmen!"

Carmen wasn't sure what she could do. Her father was still at a late council meeting, and she thought he might be a little late to the party anyway. Carmen's mother didn't drive. Carmen had her little red convertible, but Ivan lived up in the hills. The one time she had driven to his house, she was unnerved by the steep, twisting turns. She dreaded repeating that experience. "Ivan," Carmen told him, "just stay where you are, and someone will come get you."

Carmen rushed around the house looking for Lourdes. Surely Lourdes would be willing to pick up her boyfriend. She often drove up to his house. But Lourdes was nowhere to be seen. "Mama," Carmen shouted, "where's Lourdes? Ivan's car won't start, and somebody has got to get him!"

"Oh dear," Conchita Ibarra cried, "Lourdes had to run down to the store and get Ivan's birthday gift. I'm not sure when she'll get back. We could call her. But she'll never be able to get the gift, pick him up, and get back here on time."

Carmen stared at her cell phone. In a desperate moment she dialed Paul Morales.

"Yo," Paul answered.

"Paul . . .," Carmen said anxiously.

"I'm on my way, babe," Paul assured her. "I should be there in five minutes."

"Oh man, Paul," Carmen said. "I hate to ask you for such a big favor. Ivan just called, and his car won't start. He's in East County by Mount Helix, and I'd go get him. But he's up a narrow, twisting road, and I'm scared to drive up there. If somebody doesn't go get him, he'll miss his own birthday party. Could you possibly—"

"Sure doll," Paul agreed. "Just give me the address."

"Oh Paul, you're an angel," Carmen said.

At the other end of the call, Paul thought grimly: "Yeah, a reluctant angel." He didn't want to drive all the way to East County. The last person he wanted to pick up was Ivan Redondo. And Ivan was the last person he wanted riding with him for a good forty-five minutes. The guy drove Paul crazy. Besides that, Paul got the distinct impression that Ivan didn't like him and was a little afraid of him.

But Paul took the address and headed for the very upscale part of town where the Redondos lived. Ivan annoyed Paul for many reasons. Now there was another one. Paul didn't like people who lived in the hills in three-story houses where the pool house was bigger than any house in the *barrio*. Ivan Redondo was a bespectacled, rich nerd who lived in the ritzy hills. Now, on top of all that, Paul had to go out of his way—far out of his way—to bring him to a party that he didn't even want to attend. The pickup easily negotiated the steep curves until he reached the house perched atop the hill with a stunning view of the ocean many miles away.

Ivan Redondo was distraught, standing beside his disabled BMW. "Boy," he cried, "thanks for doing this, Paul! I'm really in a bind. Isn't this the pits? I heard a funny noise in the car yesterday. I guess I should've got it looked at, but I didn't. I mean, isn't this awful?"

"You said it, dude," Paul concurred. Paul surveyed the scene from the house— beautiful green canyons where other fine homes were tucked, trees and flowering shrubs, and winding driveways and sky-blue pools.

"Wow," Paul commented, "you guys got some place here. Talk about being king of the world . . ."

"My parents were very lucky in real estate," Ivan explained, scrambling to get into the small pickup.

"I'll say," Paul said.

"You don't know how much I appreciate this, Paul," Ivan raved as the small pickup turned around and started back down into the valley. "Poor little Carmen was going to come and get me. But she's afraid of driving up here. It's intimidating if you're not used to it. In fact, it even scares me."

"I can believe it," Paul mumbled under his breath.

"And Mr. Ibarra is at a council meeting," Ivan rambled on, "although I would hate to have had him come get me. Speaking of intimidating, sometimes Emilio Ibarra is a bit so, don't you think? It might be the mustache. He looks like that bandit that used to advertise potato chips until being politically correct became important and made them remove the fellow. Oh, Paul, don't ever tell Mr. Ibarra I said that. He's a wonderful man, but I wouldn't want to get on his bad side."

"Oh, my lips are sealed, dude," Paul assured him. "I *live* on Mr. Ibarra's bad side. Believe me, it ain't no fun." Paul thought to himself that no one on earth was as nerdy as this guy.

"There's a family next door here," Ivan confessed ruefully. "They have guys about my age, college guys. But do you think they would have done me a favor and driven me over to the *barrio*? They hate me, Paul."

Paul was startled by the strong term. "They *hate* you?" he repeated. Paul could easily imagine people being annoyed by Ivan Redondo. But who could actually hate such an innocuous nerd?

"Oh yes, Paul," Ivan asserted. "A lot of people my age hate me. They make fun of me." The deeply sad look on his face reminded Paul of the look that basset hounds often have when they're scolded. "You would be surprised, Paul, how many young people find me unbearable."

"No, not really," Paul said to himself. "I wouldn't be surprised 'cause I'm one of them." But to Ivan he replied, "Why is that?"

"Oh Paul, look at me," Ivan groaned. "I'm not hip or cool, or the least bit *macho*. I can be a little bit of a nerd."

"A little bit?" Paul murmured under his breath. "Dude, you are the king of nerddom."

"I wear glasses, I listen to opera music," Ivan went on. "Next door, they play that terrible rap music. When I play my opera, they get mad and smash pumpkins on our driveway. One time they almost hit me with a pumpkin they were throwing. People think rich kids are nicer than the guys who live in the *barrio*, but that's not true, Paul. Some of the rich kids get together and beat up people they don't like. Paul, you have no idea what a guy like me has gone through."

Ivan was showing a new side to Paul, who listened intently. "It's not so bad now in college," Ivan continued. "No one wants to be friends with me. But at least they're not attacking me. In the prep school where I went, they were merciless. A *macho* guy like you cannot imagine the hell I went through. I woke up every morning with stomach cramps at the thought of facing them another day."

For the first time since Paul had met Ivan Redondo, he actually felt sympathy for him. Being constantly bullied had to be awful. Paul remembered a time in middle school when some guys tried to bully him. He ended up bloodying their faces badly. In fact, they couldn't come to school the next day. He never had another problem with them.

"That's rough, Ivan," Paul said. "I hear you."

"They'd wait for me, Paul," Ivan confessed. "I'd sneak to classes by crawling behind the buildings, but they'd always find me. One day, it was in winter, and it was raining that cold drizzle we get in January. Four of them jumped me. They ripped off all my clothes and ran off with them. I was there in my shorts and socks when the English teacher at my school came along. She shrieked at me, "Ivan Redondo, what has happened to you now?""

The mental picture in Paul's mind almost made him laugh. But he didn't because he was really feeling sorry for the guy. After all, he didn't ask to be tall, skinny, and weird looking.

"That was pretty bad, Ivan," Paul told him.

"They'd even hit me with their fists, Paul," Ivan went on, glad to have a sympathetic ear. "I told my dad. But he'd just scold me and say I had to learn to fight. My father is nothing like me. He's a big, strong man. He was very disappointed in me, the way I turned out. I think he's embarrassed to have a son like me. My mom always sided with me. But you want your father's approval, and I never got that. He kept saying, 'Be a man!' But I didn't know how to do that. I made good grades, I still do, and I'm nice to people. But a lot of guys just don't respect me."

As an afterthought, it seemed, Ivan added, "I think my father is very surprised right now. Surprised that a lovely, wonderful girl like Lourdes has agreed to marry me after I finish college."

"Yeah, that's great, Ivan," Paul agreed.

"You know, Paul, I've met just one group of young men in my life who actually like and respect me. I get along fine with children and older adults. But guys my own age usually loathe me, except for these guys. I teach Bible study at my church, St. Teresa's, every Wednesday. I teach it in Spanish because many of the young guys are more comfortable with Spanish. We read the Bible and pray."

Paul tried to imagine Ivan Redondo entering a room full of tough young Hispanic guys, waiting to read the Bible and pray. It didn't make much sense. Paul tried to imagine Cruz or Beto looking at this guy and wanting anything to do with him. "So Ivan," Paul asked incredulously, "you got young guys coming to the church to listen to you talk about the Bible and pray. You got a big group?"

"I have about twenty-five in my group," Ivan answered.

"But why do they come?" Paul asked.

"It's a prison outreach, Paul," Ivan explained. "I go to the prison in South Bay and do Bible study and prayers, me and Mrs. Ibarra. I like those guys, and they seem to like me. We're not supposed to delve into what crimes got them there. But a lot of them have violent pasts. But they're kind and polite, and they don't laugh at me."

Paul gripped the steering wheel a little tighter. The last time he visited David, his brother mentioned someone. He talked about a nice young guy who came to teach the Bible. David was never religious before. But he said religion meant more to him now. He said it was the one time during the week when he felt like a normal human being, not like a convict.

"Uh . . . Ivan, is there a guy named David in your class?" Paul asked.

"Yeah," Ivan replied. "Your brother David."

Paul was shocked. "How long have you, you know, known that he's my brother?" he asked.

"Ever since we met, Paul. You guys look so much alike. I checked his name," Ivan answered.

"Let me get this straight, Ivan," Paul said. "You mean, ever since we met, you've known I got a brother in the slammer?"

"Yes," Ivan responded.

Paul turned and glanced over at Ivan. "*And you said nothing to anybody?*"

"Whom would I have told?" Ivan asked.

"Carmen, her parents, Lourdes, anybody," Paul sputtered.

"Paul, that would have been violating David's privacy," Ivan asserted. "I respect those guys. David would have been deeply hurt if I'd told your friends about him. That would have been an outrage."

Paul was stunned. Then he smiled and said, "You know what, Ivan Redondo? You're a pretty cool dude."

Ivan smiled too. "I think that's the first time in my life I've been called a 'cool dude.' It sounds great."

Paul pulled up at the house on Nuthatch Lane, and both young men got out. Carmen was there at the curb, looking anxious. Lourdes was in the front doorway, and Ivan hurried to her. For a few seconds Paul and Carmen were alone.

"Paul," Carmen told him, "thank you so much for doing this. I know it was the last thing you wanted, to be stuck with Ivan all that time—"

"No, doll," Paul objected, "actually I like Ivan. He's a good guy. I enjoyed talking to him. I got to know him, and he's real different than I thought. You know, when I got invited to this party, I felt put out having to buy a gift for the dude. I picked up an opera album. I thought, 'Why am I bothering getting this jerk something he'd like?' But now I'm happy I did that. Ivan deserves a nice gift. He's not the jerk I thought he was."

Carmen stared at Paul. "You never cease to amaze me, Paul," she declared.

"Hey, keeps life interesting, doesn't it?" Paul replied. He took Carmen's hand as they walked into the Ibarra house.

Oscar Perez played salsa and old Mexican folk tunes. The food was terrific. Once again, Abel Ruiz's food drew raves. Carmen thought the party was pretty nice. Emilio Ibarra came running in just before the food was served. Before the party ended, Lourdes and Ivan danced. So did Paul and Carmen and Emilio and Conchita Ibarra. Carmen was glad to see her father enjoying himself. He seemed to have recovered some after learning that Paul had a brother in prison.

Carmen and Paul went to the beach together on Sunday. A high pressure system had replaced the cool weather. Now it was warm and sunny. As soon as they arrived at the beach, Carmen was peeling off her sweater.

As they made their way down a rocky path to the sand, Paul took Carmen's hand. They spread a large beach towel on the sand and put the cooler on it. Carmen's mother had put together a picnic lunch with cool drinks. It was still early in the day. So they had this part of the beach almost to themselves, except for a couple farther down.

"Let's wait for the sun to get a little higher. Then it'll be warmer if we walk in the water," Paul suggested. They had worn their bathing suits to get some sun, not to swim. The water was way too cold.

"You know what, Paul?" Carmen said. "Yvette took your advice. She told Phil Serra that she'd really like to go out with him. He was real excited. They're going to see *Up*, that movie we liked so much. You don't know what you did for her, Paul. Maybe you changed her whole future by talking to her like you did."

"We lost people gotta stick together, babe," Paul declared. "The world can be pretty cruel to us. Like those nasty guys coming down on Yvette." He looked up at the sky. "Look, the clouds are going away. The sun is smiling down on us." A warm wind was blowing, and the sky filled with gulls.

"Ready?" Paul asked, stripping off his T-shirt and his jeans. He wore blue swimming trunks.

"Ready," Carmen answered. She pulled her T-shirt over her head and unwrapped her skirt. She wore a bright yellow bathing suit.

Paul looked at her and whistled. "I was right, doll," he remarked.

"Right about what?" Carmen asked him, putting her hair in a pony tail. She felt so happy with him. She felt as though she could join the gulls in the sky. All she had to do was flap her arms fast enough. She was normally a pretty happy person. But meeting Paul had given the word "happiness" a new meaning.

"Right about you being hot, doll," Paul told her.

Carmen looked at the young man in the blue trunks, at his big shoulders and impressive body. "You're pretty hot yourself, Paul Morales," she giggled.

For a while, they walked along the water's edge, the surf splashing their feet and legs.

Finally, Paul and Carmen returned to their cooler. They wrapped themselves in beach towels and sat down on the big towel. They sat there, facing the water and watching the sandpipers. The agile birds raced out with the receding water, searched for food, and then scurried back.

"Paul," Carmen said, "you told me that all the films your class made were going to be entered in a county competition. The best four would win prizes. When is that going to happen?"

"It already happened, last weekend," Paul replied, a smile on his face.

"It did?" Carmen said. He must not have done well, she thought. He would have told her if he'd won one of the prizes.

Carmen didn't want to make Paul feel bad by saying any more about it. But she did say, "Well, like my dad says, every beginning is hard. I think you got a lot of talent Paul. People are going to recognize that as you go along . . ."

Paul's jeans were neatly folded next to the picnic basket. He pulled his wallet out of the back pocket. He took a small piece of paper out and handed it to Carmen.

"Congratulations, Paul Morales. You took second prize," the card read. Second place came with a five-hundred-dollar cash prize.

"Paul," Carmen screamed, hugging and kissing him. "I'm so proud of you!"

"I get to go to Sundance too," Paul told her. Carmen screamed again, but his lips silenced her.

He kissed her and wrapped his arms around her. The sun was higher in the sky now and felt wonderfully warm. They sat quietly for a long time, watching the waves roll up on the beach.

"What're you thinking about, babe?" Paul asked softly. He was still staring at the breaking waves.

"What a wonderful guy you are," Carmen replied. "You don't have a family to fall back on. But you stick by your friends, Beto and Cruz. You stick by your brother. You almost lost him, but he'll come through all this okay, thanks to you. And you talked to Yvette and got her head turned around. She was—what was the word you used?—lost. But you brought her back."

"Yep, lost," Paul responded. "Just one lost person helpin' another. I was lost too but I'm lucky. I got found. By a great girl. You."

Carmen put her head on Paul's shoulder, and he held her a little more tightly.